A Million Angels

Kate Maryon is now officially addicted to writing!

She still walks her dog, spends as much time as she can with her children, husband and friends, works as a homeopath, runs detox retreats and does all the daily doings of a day. But there's always the possibility of a story running through her mind, the shadow of a character forming in her heart and her fingers are always itching to get back to her laptop to tippy tap away.

Kate still loves chocolate, films, eating out, reading, writing and lying on sunny beaches and she still dislikes peppermint and honey.

Scholastic $12.50

Also by Kate Maryon

Shine

Glitter

A Million Angels

Kate Maryon x

HarperCollins *Children's Books*

First published in paperback in Great Britain by HarperCollins *Children's Books* 2011
HarperCollins *Children's Books* is a division of HarperCollins*Publishers* Ltd,
77–85 Fulham Palace Road, Hammersmith, London W6 8JB

The HarperCollins *Children's Books* website address is
www.harpercollins.co.uk

1

A Million Angels
Text copyright © Kate Maryon 2011

ISBN-13 9780007326297

Typeset in AGaramond by Palimpsest Book Production Limited,
Falkirk, Stirlingshire

Printed and bound in England by
Clays Ltd, St Ives plc

For Jane, Tim, Sam, Joe & Ben,
I send a million angels to each of you every day.
Whatever you're doing, wherever you are, they fly from my heart to yours,
spinning their threads of gold, stitching us together with love.
Loving you all, for ever and always and more… and more. X

Chapter 1

Tomorrow there will be no pancakes...

Tomorrow's going to be different and I don't like different. I like things the same. The same like Dad and me. The same like peas in pods and chips off old blocks. The same like our dark curly hair, like our gunmetal grey eyes, like the little dimple on our chins. It's to do with pancakes too. My dad is the pancake king and I'm the princess. That's what Mum and Milo say, and every Sunday while we're waiting for them to get up and come downstairs we make a pile as high as Everest. Taller than the sky. The best pancakes in the world. Then we sit on the back doorstep to talk while we polish our boots. We brush and buff till they shine like silver, till we can see our eyes twinkling in the black. And we talk about everything, Dad and me. About all the mysteries inside of us. About all our wonderings of the world.

But tomorrow we won't have pancakes because my dad will be gone.

The stars are bright tonight. Glittering bursts of silver shining through midnight blue. But grey clouds are grumbling across the horizon. Rolling across the moon. Rubbing out the stars, and the wind is whisking up a storm that's sweating under my skin and heating me up with fear.

I've tried sleeping, but every time I drift off a huge eagle with sharp claws swoops down and drags me back. Then worrying images of bombs exploding everything to pieces start bouncing around again like popcorn in my brain. They pop, pop, pop and explode out of nowhere. Dark shadowy lumps that are hard to swallow. I'm trying hard to rub them out so my brain is blank and clean.

But it's impossible to stop them.

If only there was something I could do.

My phone explodes in the dark.

Pip. Pip. *U still awake?*

It's Jess. I don't really like Jess and Jess definitely doesn't like me. We're not the same kind of girl. She's all noisy and nosy, like her mum, Georgie, and I'm more quiet and like to be on my own. Well, I don't really like being on my own, of course. I would like a friend. Just not a friend like Jess – someone much more like me. But that's never going to happen because of everything about my life and how things are. So Jess and me just have to make do.

I text her back. *Yeah, can't sleep.*

Pip. Pip. *Me 2! Just can't stop thinking they might die. U know, they might never come home. It's really bad out there.*

I try swallowing the hard lump that feels like popcorn sticking in my throat, but it won't go down. I cross my fingers. I touch the little wooden table by my bed for luck.

Me 2, I text.

Pip. Pip. *We have 2 face facts, Mima... It might happen. We have 2 prepare 4 the worst. There's nothing we can do. That's what my mum keeps saying. What U doin for UR end of term presentation?*

More things smash and explode in front of my eyes, shooting worry fireworks through my veins. I *am* facing facts. I don't have any choice. I know very well that our dads might die or come back really hurt. I don't need Jess to keep rubbing it in.

Not thinking bout presentation. I hate speaking in front of every1.

Pip. Pip. *I'm really excited bout it. I want to do something really cool. Night. Hope U sleep. C U at the car boot.*

Wish I could get excited bout it, but I just get too scared. Night. I text back.

Chapter 2

His words bite me...

I creep into Milo's room. He's fast asleep with his mouth wide open like a fish. He's cuddling a toy tank, and hasn't even noticed the thunder that's raging outside. I creep downstairs to spy on my mum and dad through the crack of the open door to the sitting room. My heart is a tennis ball in my chest, pounding on concrete. My neck is sticky with sweat from the storm.

They're snuggled together on the sofa watching the late-night news. She sobs and wrings a damp hanky in her hands. He sighs and strokes her hair, twisting the threads of gold.

"*The worst year for killings since the war in Afghanistan began,*" the newsreader is saying.

On the TV screen loads of people have gathered in the street. They're watching the coffins of dead soldiers coming home from war. A woman holding flowers and crying rushes forward and presses herself against the big black hearse. She places her red, red roses on its roof and then crumples in a heap on the floor. A policewoman scurries closer and helps her up. Everyone is crying. Everything on the TV is so, so sad.

My tummy twists like my mum's wet hanky. Tying up in knots. Stopping my insides from falling out.

The thunder rumbles through me. Lightning flickers on the stairs. I start to spin so I steady myself on Dad's kit. It's been stacked in the hallway for days. He's obsessed with it. It's become his life raft on the rough and stormy sea of emotions that have been raging through our house for months. Every few hours he picks up his helmet. He smoothes it. He rocks it. He strokes it. Then he settles it back down like a precious baby nestled on top of the pile. He fusses with the straps on his bag. He straightens and sorts. He unzips and peers inside. He fiddles and straightens and sorts some more. Like a frantic bluebottle. Buzzing. Worrying. Picking at flesh. Milo loves it too. He helps with the checking.

He wanders about the house with Dad's precious helmet wobbling on top of his head.

"He's mine, remember?" I hiss at the bag. "Not yours."

Mum switches off the news. She heaves her huge dome of a belly round to face my dad. He rests his hand on it and smiles. He lowers his ear to listen to the secret baby world inside.

"Hello, little Bean," he says.

"It's so cruel," my mum says. "You've been away every time I've given birth." She grips Dad's hands and her eyes well up again. "Please come home safe, James," she says. "Please, I couldn't handle all this without you. I find Jemima so difficult when you're away. She misses you so much and tries so hard to hold it all together that she kind of closes in on herself. If I didn't know her for the sweetheart she is I'd go as far as to say that I sometimes find her behaviour quite weird. And I feel I don't do her justice. I wish I could manage her like you can. I wish I had your touch."

"Jemima's easy, Bex," he says. "She just needs a bit of reassurance, that's all. She likes to talk. To get things off her chest."

"It's all right for you," Mum sighs. "You're away. You

don't see how much she changes. To be honest, she can be really hard work when you're not here and I'm dreading it. And bless her – I know it's not her fault. She was just getting settled at school, starting to make friends, and now you going away has somehow unhinged her again. It's unhinged us all."

Unhinged? I'm not unhinged! I hate them talking about me and I know I shouldn't be spying, but I can't help it. Mum sighs.

"I don't know how much longer I can live like this, James. I have this constant worry chipping at me when you're away. You're on my mind twenty-four seven. It drives me crazy. I can't stop myself from constantly looking out of the window. It's like I'm expecting bad news. Like it would almost be a relief if it came because then the worrying would stop."

Dad runs his hand through his hair and takes hold of her hand.

"You have to get it in your head, Bex," he says, "that I've been really well trained. They wouldn't let untrained soldiers set foot in the place. It's my job to protect people, to look after those who need my help, and I do my best to do my job well. It's what I'm committed to

14

and I need you to start trusting that every day we're all doing our best to keep safe. I'm coming back home, Bex. I won't leave you. I promise."

His words bite me. I don't trust them. How can he be so sure that he'll come home safe? Like Jess says, some soldiers *do* get killed. It's a fact of war and we have to face it. I don't trust my mum either, talking about me behind my back. And I'm not *unhinged*. I can't help it that I feel safe when my dad's here and scared when he's not. I can't help it that I keep looking out of the window too and if she took the trouble to really get to know her own daughter well, then she'd know that I'm a worrier too. I wouldn't be such a puzzle for her to solve.

Mum pushes Dad away from her tummy.

"How can I trust you when we've just watched four coffins flying back from the very place you're flying out to tomorrow?" she snaps. "For God's sake, James, I'm not stupid, I know what happens in war. It's *me* you're talking to now, not the kids. Don't patronise me, *please*."

Dad looks at her and sighs. He says nothing to comfort her.

15

I creep back upstairs. If lightning strikes our house tonight my dad will keep us safe.

But not if it comes tomorrow.

Later, when the black storm rages right over our roof, my dad comes into my room. He rests his hand on my back. He rubs soft warm circles, round and round, like he did when I was small. I want to curl into him like a kitten, but I'm scared I might break like the clouds.

"I'm sleeping, Dad," I lie. "Leave me alone."

"Hey," he whispers, leaning right over me so he can see my face. "Don't do this, sweetie, not now. I know it's late, but I just wanted to check you're OK with the storm, to tell you that you're safe. I've checked all the windows and locked all the doors. Nothing's going to happen. I promise. Let's say goodbye, shall we? Just one last time."

"Don't say things like *one last time*, OK?"

I turn over to look at him and drink him in like an ice-cold lemonade on a hot summer's day. I must never forget him. The dark whiskers sprouting from his chin. The map of blue veins like motorways on his hands. The puddle of curry stain yellowing his shirt. The waft of smelly underarm odour that's drifting up my nose. I must memorise him, just in case... and I'll keep him safe and undisturbed in a beautiful heart room where he'll shimmer in the light.

"Don't go, Dad," I squeak. "Please?"

"I have to, sweetie," he says, nuzzling tickly whiskers in my neck. He plants a kiss on my cheek. "Promise me you'll take good care of yourself? And be kind to Milo and really good for Mum? I need you to be a big girl and look after her for me while I'm away. She's got a lot going on with the baby coming. She'll need your help, Mima, so try not to stress her out, OK?"

I nod even though I don't want to. At least my dad understands me.

"Good girl. I'm leaving really early in the morning so I won't wake you again."

When he leaves my room I touch his kiss and wish it would grow into a flower.

At five the next morning my dad creeps into my room. I lie still and hold my breath. He pulls my duvet up to my chin and strokes my hair. He gives me one last clean-shaven kiss and creeps away. My tummy sinks. It sinks right through the bed and through the floor, and as if a huge crack in the earth has opened up I feel like I'm falling, falling, falling into a deep black hole.

"Please don't go," I whisper.

I hear him in the other rooms. Now he's going down the stairs and into the hall. I hear scrapes and scuffs and clunks and I know he's putting on his sparkling black boots, shuffling his kit about and loading it on to his back. I hear someone hug him. Then the front door clicks shut and I freeze. My hand flies to my cheek, to his kiss where the flower didn't grow. I jump out of bed and race like lightning down the stairs. I open the front door and step out into the storm. A soldier with a silver car salutes my dad. A river of rain runs down his sleeve.

"Dad!" I call.

My dad spins round.

"Jemima! Sweetie! You're getting soaked!"

"I don't care," I say, paddling up to him. "Dad, please don't go. Please don't leave me. Afghanistan is too far away. I just need to be near you."

"Oh, darling," he sighs. "As much as I'd love to stay, I have to go, you know that. Let's not make it any harder than it already is, eh?"

"But, Dad," I whisper, "what if something bad happens. There might be a fire or a burglar. Or someone might get hurt. We might need you."

"Mima," he says, "this is why I didn't wake you, sweetheart. It's much easier if I just slip away."

"Not for me it isn't," I say. "Just one more hug then?"

And Dad scoops me into his arms as if I were a tiny toddler. He squeezes me so tight I think my lungs might burst out of my chest and splat down on the floor. We're not crying, but tears from the thundering black storm clouds soak us through and settle like diamonds on our lashes. We find each other's eyes and tie a knot in our gaze.

"Love you, pipsqueak," Dad says. He kisses my nose.

"Love you, Lieutenant Colonel Taylor-Jones."

He stands me down. We salute one another. The soldier drives my dad away.

The rain puddles between my toes and bounces off my skin. My tummy sinks through the tarmac road, through the earth's muddy crust, right down to the blackest, darkest hole at the bottom of the world. I can't let him go. I can't. I run after the car. I shout.

"Dad, quick, stop!" He moves further and further away. "Dad, please, stop! Please!"

The road is empty. I leap into the middle and wave my arms like mad.

"Dad!" I call.

At last, the red brake lights go on and the soldier reverses the car until it's level with my feet.

"What is it, Mima?"

I stand frozen like a dummy in the road, with a million words raining on my mind.

"I… erm…" I stumble. "I… I… What would make you come back home, Dad? I mean, how bad a thing would have to happen?"

My face is soaked with rain. He can't see my tears.

"I'm so sorry, sweetheart," he says, checking his watch. "I haven't got time to talk about it now – everyone's waiting for me. But I promise you you'll be OK. Everything will be fine. Mum's here, Granny's here and I'll be home for a two-week R & R break before you know it. Then my tour will be halfway done, Mima, and then I'll be back home for good."

"Until they send you away again," I sigh.

Dad salutes me one last time.

"Trust, Mima, trust."

The soldier drives him away and my words tumble like rocks through the air.

"I'm scared you're going to die, Dad. I'm scared you're never coming home."

Chapter 3

My tongue is itching to ask...

The house feels so quiet without Dad and the hall is too empty without his mountain of kit getting in the way. My mum and Milo are still sleeping, but Granny is in the kitchen sipping tea. We had a leaving party yesterday for Dad, and Granny moved in. She's here to help Mum with the baby when it comes.

"You listen to me, James," she'd said to my dad, shaking his shoulders hard, "and make sure you come home safe, see. There'll be big trouble if you don't, do you hear me? I've lost too many people in my life to be doing with losing you."

"Don't you worry, Ma," he said, folding her paper-thin body into his arms. "I'll be back."

I creep upstairs, wrap myself in a towel, then go back down and watch Granny from the doorway. She blows and sips hot tea. Thought bubbles float over her head. I like spying on people when they don't know I'm looking. People act differently when they think they're on their own.

"Hello, pet," she says. "You startled me. You're up early. Do you want some tea?"

I don't really like tea, but I like chatting with Granny. I nod and climb on the chair next to hers.

"I heard Dad," I say, "and needed another hug. I wish he didn't have to go."

"I know, pet," she says, pouring my tea. "You'll get used to it soon enough. It was the same with your grandpa; he was always off here and there and everywhere. All over the place he was. That's army life for you, see."

"I don't like it," I say. "I wish he had a normal job. What happens if we need him, Granny? Do you think he'd come back home if one of us got really ill, or the house burned down or someone died?"

"If something really bad happened, Mima," she says,

patting my hand, "then they'd send him home. You can be sure of that. But I promise you we won't need him. We'll manage and it'll be fun with the baby coming." She sighs. "Army life is in his bones, pet. He wouldn't settle to a normal job. And people have to do what's in their bones."

"Well, I wish he had something else in his bones,' I sigh. "He could do anything else except this."

"You'll understand it one day," says Granny. "You'll get an itch in your bones and you'll be off out in the world doing what you love."

"I won't," I say. "I'm never leaving home. It's too scary and I can't even decide what to do my end of term presentation on, let alone know what I want to do when I grow up. And I hate presentations, Granny. They're so pointless and I'm so rubbish at them. My voice always goes all wobbly and I end up looking like a stupid red beetroot. I wish school couldn't make you do stuff you hate."

"Ooh!" says Granny, leaping up. "I just remembered. I've got something for you that might help."

She creaks her granny bones upstairs to her room and comes down with a dusty old box in her hands.

"Here," she says. "I found this when I was clearing out my things ready to move into my new flat. I thought you might be interested. You know, family history and all. Maybe you'll find something in there to inspire you for your presentation."

I rummage through Granny's dusty box. There are some really old letters, some faded photographs and a million old-fashioned stamps that have been carefully torn from envelopes. There are some documents that look like they should be on display in a museum and odd bits of ribbon and spare buttons and all sorts of random stuff that's made this box its home. The envelopes have black handwriting on them where spiders with inky feet have danced. I love the photos. They're so funny and black and white and old.

"It's all interesting, Granny," I say, sifting through the things, "but how do I turn a box of stuff into a presentation?"

"Give it a bit of thought and something'll come to you, I'm sure. Oh, look," she says, pointing to a photo of a little girl in a white dress standing next to a big black dog. "That's me and my dog, Buster; I must only have been about three years old."

I turn the photo over. The spider has written, *Dorothy and Buster, 1934 – Bognor Regis*. Then I find another of Granny holding a baby in her arms, which says, *Dorothy and Joan, 1937*.

"Who's Joan?" I ask.

Granny wipes a tear from her pale watery eyes. "She was my baby sister," she says. "She died in the Blitz along with the rest of them. She was only three. She was a beauty, she was; she stole my heart right away, the moment she was born."

"What happened?" I ask.

"It's too painful to talk about, Mima. It was 1940 and I was nine years old. The Blitz began and I lost my whole world in a day. My home, my family and a very dear friend."

"How come?"

"Bombs," she says, getting up. She fusses with the cups. "The whole house was destroyed in the blast. The entire street. Gone!"

Her hands tremble at the kitchen sink. Her china cup chinks against the tap.

"But what happened to *you*, Granny?" I ask. "Weren't you scared, being left all alone?"

"Leave it, pet," she sighs. "There's a good girl."

"But Granny…"

"I said leave it, pet. It still upsets me, see, even after all these years."

"But I can't just stand up in class and say, 'Oh, well, this is my granny's old box full of interesting stuff that I don't know anything about. The End.' Can I?"

"Just look at the bits and bobs, pet," she says, "and get a bit inspired. I'll tell you more when I'm ready."

I look through the photos for clues. There are loads of photos of fat old women. They have sour faces. They're wearing long dresses and heavy hats pulled right down over their eyebrows. There are some young men wearing stripy bathing suits and cheesy smiles, but there's no sign of anything Blitz-ish. There's a row of girls in matching black costumes with white swimming caps on and pegs on their noses, and another of a very old man with a beard so long it's tucked in his belt. There's one photo of two girls, one looks about twelve, like me, and the other a bit older. They're wearing summer dresses and short white socks. They're sitting on a shingly beach, laughing and eating delicate sandwiches and huge chunks of cake. On the back the spider has danced, *Barbara and Sonia, 1938 – Bognor Regis*.

There's a photo of a young woman with dark curly hair like Dad's and mine. She's wearing a white wedding dress and standing next to a soldier with a quiff. They're holding hands and their smiles are like sunshine lighting up their eyes. On the back the spider has scrawled, *Kitty and James, 1917 – London*.

I hold the photo up for Granny to see. But I'm careful not to ask questions in case I make her cry.

"My parents," she says, peering at the photo. "Your great-grandparents. Their wedding day that was, pet, and look – you've got her hair. Same as your dad too."

I fiddle with my curls. I twirl a dark lock round and round my finger. I press my thumb over my great-grandmother's face and her curls bubble out at the sides.

I want to know what happened.

My tongue is itching to ask.

Tucked in one corner of the box is a little red Bible. It's so tiny I can hold it in one hand and the print is so miniscule I have to squint my eyes to read what it says. The spidery scrawl on the inside cover is big though, and reads, *James Taylor-Jones, 29 Sept 1917. From Miss Perks, Soldiers' Homes, Winchester.*

"So this was your dad's then?" I ask. "My great-grandfather's?"

Granny smiles. "That's right," she says. "I managed to rescue it when... well, you know when."

"I wish I did know, Granny," I say, "but I don't because you won't tell me anything, remember? I wish you'd given it to Dad. It might have kept him safe."

"Didn't do a lot for my father," she says, "did it?"

"Don't you believe in the Bible and God and stuff then?" I ask.

Granny sighs, plonks a fresh pot of tea and a huge pile of toast on the table and sits back down.

"That's a hard question, Mima, when you've had a life like mine," she says. "It's one of the many questions that have been puzzling me since I was nine. If there is a God, see, then why does He let such bad things happen all the time?"

I nod and stir my tea. I haven't really thought about it before. I sing along with all the hymns in assembly and I mumble along with the prayers. But I've never wondered before if I actually believe in the words.

"I heard Mum say last night that when Dad's away it's like she's waiting for bad news. Like the bad news would be better than the waiting," I say, "and I understand her. I wish there was something I could do, Granny. Something to make certain that he comes back home."

"Life's never certain, Mima," says Granny. "We can never tell what's round the corner; I should know. You just have to trust, see. Live for today and get on with loving as best you can. None of us knows how long we've got."

"When Dad left, he said, 'Trust, Mima, trust,' but what do you both mean?"

"I never managed to answer the God question," Granny says, "so I eventually settled on trusting in life and trusting what feels true in me. There's not a lot else you can do. You have to trust that life will work out in its own mysterious way. That's the beauty of it."

"Well, *I'm* not leaving it to life to work it out," I say. "*I'm* going to find a way to bring him back and *then* I'm going to find a way of making sure he never leaves again. Jess keeps saying bad things; she keeps saying our dads might die and that wouldn't be mysterious, Granny, that would just be sad."

Granny tuts.

"She's trouble, that one," she says. "You can see it in her eyes. Don't listen to her, pet. Keep your thoughts on the bright side."

I turn the red Bible in my hand and think about how to make all these pictures and stuff into a presentation and am just about to put it back in the box when a small photo of a boy drops out. His face is solemn. His eyes are big and soft. I flip the photo over, looking for where the spider scrawled his name, but it's blank.

"Who's this, Granny?" I ask.

Her watery eyes sparkle like Christmas.

"There he is," she smiles. "I've been searching everywhere for *him*. This is the friend I lost."

She takes the photo from me and plants a kiss on the face of the boy.

"You cheeky thing," she says to the boy, "hiding all this time."

"Who is he?" I ask.

"Him?" she smiles. "He's Derek, my childhood sweetheart. We used to have so much fun together."

She sifts through the box and pulls out the photo of the two girls on the beach.

"These were his sisters," she says, "Barbara and Sonia. They disappeared too. It was all a bit of nonsense really, but we were such good friends. And Derek and I had something special. We shared a birthday, and the war did strange things to us all. People got married at the drop of a hat and we just got caught up in the spirit of it. We were only children, but we crossed our hearts and vowed to be sweethearts for ever. We started making all these silly promises and then *poof* – like magic he disappeared. I never ever saw him again. See what I mean – you never know for certain what's going to happen. But think on it, if I'd have married Derek then I wouldn't have met your grandpa and Daddy wouldn't have had you. Trust life, Jemima; flow with its mystery."

A single diamond tear tips on to her cheek.

"But it would've been nice to hear from him again. Just once. Just to know what happened." She laughs. "You're a smart one. Determined to get me talking."

"Do you think he's dead, Granny?" I say.

"Probably by now, pet."

Chapter 4

I'm going to collect these...

After breakfast, Mum starts getting ready for the car boot sale.

"You go with Milo," I say, "and leave me here with Granny. I hate hanging out with Jess."

Mum gives me her beady eye that means, 'Please do as you're told, Jemima, because I am not so full of patience.' But I ignore it. I do not want to do as I'm told. I do not want to go to the car boot sale!

"Don't start, Mima," she says. "Not today."

I have a beady eye too, but I wait until her back is turned before I give it to her.

Milo clings on to my leg.

"Please come, Mima," he says. "Please come! Please come! Please come!"

He hangs off me like I'm a tree and twists the skin on my leg.

"Mima! Mima! Mima!" he chants like I'm a football match that needs cheering on.

"Ouch, Milo," I say. "You're hurting me!"

"I said, don't start, Mima!" says Mum. "Today is hard enough for us all without you making things worse."

When she turns her back I poke out my tongue. I wish I could stand up and say, YOU'RE THE ONE WHO IS UNHINGED, MUM. But I don't. The things I really want to say always get choked up in my throat until I'm forced to swallow them down. It's the same with Jess. She says worrying stuff that frightens me, she gossips with her mum and tells me stuff my ears don't want to hear. So many times I want to say, SHUT UP, JESS! But as hard as I try I just can't.

I hope one day my voice will unblock itself like a drain and I'll be able to speak up so clearly, like LALALALAALLLAAAA! Then everyone will hear everything that's all blocked up inside.

* * *

It's heaving at the car boot sale. Everyone shoves and pushes in search of pathetic old treasures and silly magical gems. Milo has a pound burning in his fist. He rummages through buckets and baskets of wrecked toy cars looking for trucks and tanks.

"Look, Mima," he says, holding up a rusty old tank. "Isn't it great? D'you think Dad drives one like this?"

Jess bounces around like a spaniel looking for strokes. She tries to act cool and flirts her fringe when we pass a stall with boys selling a few broken old skateboards. Jess is as pathetic as the car boot sale. I wish we could put her on a stall and sell her, but I'd feel sorry for the poor family who ended up buying her. They'd be really disappointed, even if they only paid fifty pence for her.

I wouldn't buy her for a penny. I wouldn't even want Jess for free, even if she was going to be my slave.

I look at my watch. I wish I was at home. Thinking.

"Calm down, Jess," says Georgie. "Oooh... Mima, what do you think of Jess's new jacket? We got it yesterday. Isn't it just so pink!"

"Erm..." I say, bending down to tie the lace on one of my big black boots. "Yes, Georgie, it's definitely pink."

"I think it's gorgeous," says Mum. "You should try

35

something like this, Mima. You know... a bit pretty. Get yourself out of those boots for a change. Look," she says, shoving a ten-pound note in each of our hands, "why don't you girls go off together and see what you can find?"

I glare at Mum. I don't want to be left with Jess. And she knows that! I'd rather look after Milo. I'd rather wander around alone.

I flash my eyes at Mum, trying to say, DON'T LEAVE ME WITH JESS. But she ignores me and shoos us both away. I bet her and Georgie want to talk about our dads. In private!

Jess slides over to the skateboard boys.

"Hi," she says, twiddling with her fringe. She picks up a cruddy old board. "How much for this?"

"A fiver," says one of the boys.

Jess flashes her eyes at them.

"That's a rip-off," she says, pulling me away. "We had a huge sigh of relief this morning when my dad finally left," she smiles. She opens her arms wide and takes a deep breath. "It's going to be bliss. I can't actually believe we have six whole months without him shouting and bossing us around."

She rummages through a pile of old clothes. She pulls out her purse and pays for a pair of shiny black high heels that are two sizes too big. She holds up a pink dress covered in gold sequins.

"What d'you think?"

"Mmmm," I say. "It would match your jacket but…"

"I don't even know why I bother asking your opinion," she huffs, holding it up for size. "It's not as if you're Miss Fashionista, is it, Jemima? That enormous Minnie Mouse bow in your hair and those big black boots aren't exactly a major fashion statement, you know! And as for the rainbow nail varnish! Whatever crazy thing are you going to buy today? A granny jacket? Another big bow?"

"I'm looking for something," I say, "but I'm not sure what. I'll know when I see it."

She throws the dress down and we drift on to the next stall.

"Don't you miss your dad at all when he's away?" I ask.

"Not At All!" she says. "It's our little secret, but Mum and me prefer it when he's away. We get up to mischief. Last time we went on this amazing spa day pamper thing and we had a massage and our nails done and we lounged around in the Jacuzzi for hours. Then we went for dinner at this gorgeous restaurant. My dad hates restaurants and mealtimes are horrible when he's around. He makes me sit up straight and hold my knife properly and boring stuff like that. I love it when it's just Mum and me and I get all her attention. This time we're planning a mini-break to a really lovely hotel in Paris so we can shop, shop, shop. My dad's not Mr Perfect like *your* dad, is he? *My* dad's always really moody and bossy and he shouts all the time. I feel sorry for the soldiers he's in charge of. Rather them than me."

"I can't stop thinking about mine," I say. "It's like I have this little bubble of worry following me around. I worked out exactly how long they're going to be away for. Six months equals twenty-six weeks. That means one hundred and eighty-two days, or four thousand, three hundred and eighty hours, or two hundred and sixty-two thousand, eight hundred minutes, or fifteen million, seventy-seven hundred and thirty-eight thousand and four hundred seconds. That's ages. It's too long."

"Not long enough for me," she says. "I can't believe you bothered to work all that out. Even worse, you

38

bothered to remember it. You're nuts, Jemima. You need to learn to switch off and think about nice things. Like me and Mum do." She giggles. "Plan something special."

"How can you think of *nice* things," I say, "when you know your dad might get killed?"

"Well, soldiers do get killed," she says, "like I said last night, it's a fact. But worrying won't help. It's not as if there's anything *you* can do to stop it. Anyway," she says with a smug little smile, "nothing'll kill *my* dad. Mum and I think he's so stubborn he'd even survive a nuclear war!"

"You can't say that," I snap. "You can't be that sure. And he definitely wouldn't survive a nuclear attack, Jess, that's just stupid. No one would survive that."

Something sparkly catches her eye and she skips along to a stall full of junk. While I wait for her to coo at dusty old ornaments of leaping dolphins and sad-looking bears my eye fixes on a stall. It has green camouflage and combat gear all piled up high. And there's a helmet snuggled like a baby on the top.

"I'll be back in a bit," I say. I push through the crowd. I can see something hanging from a railing, swinging in the rain.

"Wait for me," Jess calls. "Hang on."

The stall is amazing. It's piled to the sky with all things war. There are jackets and bags and flasks and green camp beds. There are big metal boxes and old radio equipment and belts and buckles and caps and hats and shiny medals in boxes and posters and books and...

"This," I say, pulling it off the railing. "How much for this?"

"I'll throw in the original box," says the beardy man, "this little brown suitcase and a few of these old wartime posters and you can have the lot for a tenner."

"Done!" I smile.

"What d'you want *those* for?" asks Jess, catching me up.

"I like them."

Jess frowns. She shows me her new collection of plastic dolphins. They have sparkling sprays of glitter running down their silky grey backs.

"I'm going to collect them," she smiles.

"I'm going to collect these," I glare.

On the way home Milo takes his tanks into battle up and down the car seat and Jess swoops her dolphins through the air so they look like they're swimming and leaping in the sea. My mum is fuming. I think she wishes the dolphins were mine. But I think she's unfair. You can't really give someone money and then get cross about how they spend it. A gift is a gift, after all.

"I just don't understand why you'd want to buy anything so ridiculous, Mima," she says when we get back home. "I give you ten pounds to spend on something *nice* to cheer you up, something *pretty*... and you waste it on stuff like *this*. Why didn't you buy lovely dolphins like Jess. Or something cute to wear?"

She swings my gas mask from her finger.

"Well, I happen to like my things," I say, snatching it back. "And I don't think they're a waste of money. Dad would understand. Anyway, they're for my end of term presentation. They're for school. You should be pleased."

I run upstairs and cradle the gas mask in my hands. I stroke its big glass fly eyes. War is a mystery to me, another of the great mysteries of the world. I hang the gas mask on the end of my bed, pull down my Hello Kitty posters and replace them with the army ones. I run along the hall to the airing cupboard and dig around in the pile, looking for Dad's old camouflage duvet cover that he had in Iraq. If I'm going to do my presentation on Granny's old Blitz box, I need to get myself into the mood.

At one o'clock it's time to go over to the mess for the monthly Sunday lunch. It's different here without my dad. I didn't want to come. I wish my mum would understand me and leave me alone.

Milo charges along the road with a stick in his hand, holding it like a gun.

"Piiiiiooowwww! Piiiiioooooow!" he goes. "I'm gonna kill all the baddies, Mum," he says. "I'm gonna beat the world and win the war. I'm gonna chop all the nasties' heads off, then Dad can come back home."

That sets Milo off thinking about Dad. He stands still. His bottom lip trembles. He opens his mouth wide.

"I waaaaannnttt my dad!" he yells. "I waaaaannnttt my daaaaaaddd!"

Mum huffs. She pulls him into her arms.

"It's OK, Milo," she says. "Dad will come home soon, I promise."

Milo snuffles and snots in her hair. He loops his arms round her neck.

"Chin up!" says Granny, and she starts twittering away like a mad old bird. "Chin up and put your best foot forward. Settle down for a nice cup of tea. That's what we used to say in the war." Then she wanders into the mess like she's in a dream, like she's not even on the same planet as us any more.

Milo follows Granny with his big blue eyes. Then he looks at Mum.

"Carry?" he whispers.

"I can't manage you, darling," she says. "Not in this state. I'm so sorry."

"But my legs won't work," he cries. "I need a caaaarrrrryyy!"

Mum sighs. She rubs her enormous belly and looks at me.

"Can you manage him for me, Mima, sweetheart? He's so upset. I can't do it and Granny clearly can't. I don't know what's got into her today. It's like she's been transported to another world. I hope she's not going to go all Alzheimer-ish on us. That's all I need!"

I know what's wrong with Granny and it's not Alzheimer's, it's Derekheimer's, and no one knows but me that she's hiding the photo of him in her bra. I don't

43

say anything about it to Mum. It's Granny's secret. And mine. I pull Milo into my arms, heave him up on my hip and whisper into his ear.

"I'm thinking hard, Milo," I say. "I'm planning a Bring Dad Home mission and I promise you he'll be home soon!"

"Come on," says Mum. "Let's get some lunch, shall we? We're all just hungry and tired and overwrought."

She rests her hand on my back and rubs soft warm circles.

"I know it's hard, Mima," she whispers. "I don't really feel like being here either, but we have to go. We have to keep up appearances. For Dad. And sometimes the support of everyone helps, you know, because we're all going through the same thing."

She tucks a curl behind my ear.

"Like Granny says, chin up!" she laughs, guiding us in. "Chin up, and remember to be polite."

While Mum greets everyone with her fake smile and chats about when the Bean's due and how bad her backache is and how hard it is for her to sleep, Milo and I are forced to stand next to her and smile. Red puckered kisses land on our cheeks like planes. Perfume chokes us like fire. I wish I were brave enough to stand on a chair and make an announcement. THEY ALL MIGHT DIE! I want to say. THEY SHOULD BE HOME HERE, WITH US, EATING ROAST BEEF! HAVEN'T YOU NOTICED THAT THEY'VE GONE?

My dad and the other soldiers have barely even said goodbye and it feels like everyone but me has already bleached them away. Everyone is chattering and laughing like normal. The gaps at the tables where they should be sitting are filled with bright fake laughter that's shrieking through the air and shattering it like glass. I wish I were young like Milo. I wish I could stand up and have a tantrum and say, I WAAAANNNTTTT MY DAAAAADDD! I'd love to see the look on everyone's faces if I did and if I were brave enough, I would. I promise you. I'd open my mouth and let the words tumble right out.

I try. I open my mouth wide.

Hoping.

But the sounds just jumble and crash in my throat.

My dad is probably still on his plane and I wonder what he's having for his lunch. He's up there somewhere in the storm clouds. On his way to Afghanistan. I know he'll be waiting until it's dark. Until it's time to put his helmet and body armour on and for the lights to black out so the plane can dive towards the ground, unseen. Until the heavy desert smells and heat rise and swallow him up him for six whole months.

I've seen it happen in some of Dad's films. I shouldn't really, but I sneak them from the shelf sometimes and watch them on my laptop, under my covers, at night. In one of them all the soldiers rushed off the plane with their guns poking out from under their arms. Their heads twitched around, looking for danger and then piiiaaaooooww, like Milo does, the guns started shooting and bodies were everywhere, flying through the air.

I can't believe that all this might be happening to my dad while we're here waiting for lunch. It doesn't seem real. It doesn't seem right.

I pick at my lunch. I'm not really hungry. Mum and Georgie huddle together and talk in whispers. Granny is lost in her dream. I have to chop up Milo's meat and play trains with his veg. Jess is opposite me. She scoffs her food like usual with her big fat stupid grin.

"I've got big plans for my presentation," she says, whooshing her dolphins through the air, dunking their snouts in her gravy. "Have you decided what you're doing yours on yet?"

I glare at her.

"I've got more important things on my mind, Jess," I say. "More important things like my dad."

"You're boring, Mima," she says. "Get over yourself. He'll either come back alive or he'll come back dead!" She slurps a piece of floppy beef into her mouth. "Nothing much we can do about it. But he'll be back one way or another. Shame my dad has to come back at all."

I cover Milo's ears.

"Please don't say the D.E.A.D. word in front of Milo," I whisper. "You'll set him off crying again."

"I'll say what I want," Jess glowers. "You're not the boss of me, Jemima Taylor-Jones."

Then she storms off to get pudding.

After lunch, Milo charges about with some little ones playing war. He uses his fingers to make a gun.

"Piiiiooooowww! Piiiiooooowwwww! Piiiiooooowww!"

The noise saws into my brain. I wish they would just stop and sit down and do some colouring or something peaceful like that. A red chubby-cheeked baby on another table starts crying and crying and crying and his mum ignores him and keeps chatting on and on and on. Everyone's voices are screeching and battling with each other and I wish I could scream out loud and say, STOP!!!! SHUT UP!!!!!! BE QUIET!!!!!

I slide closer to Mum.

"Can we go soon, Mum? Please!" I whisper. "I'm so bored."

"I'm not ready to leave yet, Mima," she shouts above the din, drowning me with custard breath. "I'm having fun."

"But how can you have fun," I say, "when Dad's only just gone away? And you didn't even want to come yourself. You said!"

"Because what else am I supposed to do, Jemima?" she hisses. "I have to be here, and if I let myself go I'll end up in a puddle of tears and I won't be able to stop for the next six months. And what good would that do? So I'm *trying* to get on and have fun. I'm well aware that Dad's gone and I don't need *you* to keep reminding me of that fact every five minutes. I'm just trying to put a brave face on it – we all are…"

She cradles her fat belly in her hands and her voice cracks open.

"I know you're hurting too, Jemima, and I'm sorry that it's so hard for you when he goes, but going on about it isn't going to help." She digs around in her bag and pulls out my iPod. "If you're that bored listen to this, or go and talk to Jess, because we're not leaving yet."

I fire invisible bullets at her. I'd rather be facing possible death in Afghanistan with my dad than be stuck here with her and Milo and the fat greedy baby in her tummy.

I slide over to Granny.

"I'm bored, Granny," I say. "I want to go home."

Granny smiles at me, but she's not really here. She's lost in her memories of Derek and Bognor Regis and the Blitz.

She pats my arm.

"Listen to your music for a bit, pet," she smiles. "Like Mum said."

I get another helping of apple crumble and custard and plug myself into Kiss Twist and as soon as they start singing 'A Million Angels' I know I've discovered the first part of my Bring Dad Home mission.

I dig around in Mum's bag, find a biro and a felt-tip

pen and set to work on my skin. I draw a million angels up and down my arms and blow them to my dad. I watch them flutter from my skin and fade from biro blue to a radiant flash of brilliant white wings that swoop and soar through the sky. I watch a million angels settle around him so they can guard him and keep him safe until I can find a way to bring him back home.

I just finish linking the angels together with a string of tiny red felt-tip pen hearts when a little girl sits next to me and holds out her arm.

"Want some angels too?" I ask. "For your dad?"

"For my mum," she whispers, her eyes twinkle with tears. "She went away this morning, before I was awake."

"Same as my dad," I say.

I draw a million inky angels up and down her little arms and string them together with hearts.

"You have to blow them through the sky to your mum. Look," I say, blowing the first one for her. "Watch them fly."

And one by one the angels flutter from her arms and soar towards the sky. The little girl swallows and opens her eyes wide.

"They're really going to find her?" she says.

"Really," I say. "I promise. And they're going to look after her too. They're going to keep her safe. They're going to bring her home."

I begin working my way around the dining room. I draw a million inky angels and felt-tip pen hearts up and down all the kids' arms. Everyone wants some, except Jess. She glares at me. She swoops her plastic glittery dolphins through the air. But I won't let her stop me. I keep going and going and other kids start drawing too until we're a frenzied army of blue biros. A battalion of red felt-tipped pens.

"You're all crazy," says Jess, "if you really think pathetic biro angels are going to help. It's not a game our dads are playing, Jemima, they're fighting a war!"

"But maybe if we draw enough of them," I say, "and we all keep blowing them every day, it might help. Just imagine how many of them are flying through the sky right now. There must be a trillion at least. My dad told me about this thing called collective thought. It's a powerful thing, Jess. It's when lots of people are thinking hard about the same thing to try to make something happen. Maybe it's a bit like when people pray for peace and stuff and for everyone to be saved. And you don't know, it might just work because miracles do happen, you know."

Jess raises her eyebrows and laughs.

"But they're not flying, are they?" she says, staring at our arms. "They're just pictures, Mima. Useless biro pictures."

I swallow the lump in my throat, ignore her horrid words and turn back to the other kids.

"Don't listen to Jess, listen to me. You have to keep blowing them," I say. "Every single day and I promise all our dads and mums will come home safe. *Everyone* will come home alive."

A shadow falls over my face.

"Jemima!" my mum shrieks, towering over me. "What on earth are you doing?"

The shrill and tinkling laughter clatters and smashes to the ground. Everyone's sharp eyes and dazzling lips land on me.

"Look at them all," she says, pointing to the inky octopus of arms. "It'll take for ever to wash all that off, Jemima, and everyone has school in the morning."

"I was only trying to help," I say. "I thought it was a lovely idea."

"It might be a lovely idea, sweetheart," she sighs, "but it isn't really helping, is it? Helping is being good and getting on with things."

Later, when I'm alone in bed, the wind howls around the house. Hisses through the window frames, roars through the trees. Thunder growls in the distance again. Rumbling this way.

I creep out of bed and along the hall to Granny's room. She's propped up on a tower of pillows. She snores in her dreams. I slide under her cover, find a warm spot and snuggle down. I trace the angels on my arm with my finger and think about my mum. I wish she'd understand me more, like my dad does. He'd understand that I *am* trying to help. He'd understand that my angels are *my* way of getting on with things.

Chapter 5

You'll be in for the chop, I promise...

In the morning, when Mum's busy in the kitchen, I creep into her room, open Dad's wardrobe and climb inside. I burrow through the forest of fabric and snatch a deep noseful of his smell. I shut my eyes and he's right here next to me, reaching out for my hand. I search for his, but all I find are the ghosts of empty jacket sleeves, the wood of the wardrobe that reminds me of coffins and dead soldiers on TV. The ghosts shudder through me like silk slipping over my skin. I reach up to the top shelf and pull down one of Dad's berets, then I creep back to my room. I tuck my gas mask in my bag and shove my school shoes under the bed. I shout goodbye and head off towards the bus before Mum sees what I'm wearing.

I hate the school bus. Everyone huddles together in cosy little groups and I never know where to sit. I wish I could camouflage with the grey seats or turn myself into a window. Then everyone could sit on me or peer through me, but not see me. They could get cosy on me or draw hearts in my window mist and things like that.

I pull a notebook out of my bag and make myself look busy. Mrs Cassidy wants us to get all our presentation ideas on paper so we can tell the whole class what we're planning before we do our research. I'm going to use Granny's box because I can't think of anything else to do it on. I want it to be all about Granny and Derek. I want to show people that war doesn't only bomb things and kill people. War also breaks hearts. I want to make it sad and touching. I want my audience to cry.

Mrs Cassidy is going to love it. Granny's going to love it. And if Derek isn't dead I think he'll love it too. That's why I need to start my Bring Derek Home mission right away. Granny needs him like I need Dad and if I don't bring them both back the war will have won and everyone will end up dying with a broken heart. And that would be too sad.

That is, of course, if I'm still at school by the end of term.

Part two of my Bring Dad Home mission is brewing nicely inside, but it doesn't need writing on paper, it's written on my heart.

At the very top of the first page I write *END OF TERM PRESENTATION* and underline it in red felt-tip pen. Then I write the word *WAR*, which makes the images from Dad's war films dance about in my brain, and my tummy flips.

I stuff my notebook in my bag. I can't bear to look at it any more. It's the word 'war' I hate. It stings me. I stroke a little angel that's peeping out from under my sleeve and blow it to Dad. I watch it flurry from my skin, shaking its wings. Fading from biro blue to a radiant flash of brilliant white, a blaze of pure beauty that swoops and soars towards the sky. It flies over the seas and the oceans. It sweeps through the clouds and the stars. It heads straight, like a dart, to the heat of the desert that's frying under the sun.

Then I blow a million more and watch them settle

all around him, guarding him, keeping him safe until my plan works out and I can bring him back home.

Jess bounces on the bus with a big smile.

"Hi," she says, plonking herself next to me. "Have you heard from him yet?"

I shake my head.

"Neither have we. We've been watching the news though," she says. "My mum's eyes are practically glued to it. All sorts of terrible things are happening, Jemima. There've been bombs already! Mum says they really will be lucky if they make it home this time. Imagine! This might be it!"

She grips my arm.

"We might be on telly!"

I wish I could stand on the bus seat with a megaphone and shout, SHUT UP! I'd like to say it really, really loudly, just like that, so that everyone would hear. I'd like to take my socks off and stuff them in Jess's mouth and say, SHUT UP, JESS. JUST STOP TALKING ABOUT SCARY STUFF, OK? SHUT UP! That would make me really happy. But I keep my mouth closed and flick a little tiny angel from my wrist towards the sky.

"Why are you wearing your dad's beret?" she says.

"Jemima, you are so weird. You do know that, don't you? And if Mrs Bostock catches sight of you wearing those boots, or catches a glimpse of that angel mess up your arms, you'll be in for the chop, I promise."

"She can chop me up as fine as an onion," I say. "See if I care. Being dead would be fine by me. At least I wouldn't have to go to her stupid school any more. I don't really care about anything, Jess, except getting my dad back home. And that's the truth."

I turn away from her and stare out at the rain. Everything is grey. Even the houses are sad. It is true. I don't care about anything else but my dad and Derek and bringing them safely home.

"If you're just going to be boring and stare out the window," says Jess, leaping up, "I'm off."

She bounces to the back of the bus and slides on to a seat next to Ned Cotsford. She giggles. I stare at the rain. Life would be so much easier if I were a raindrop. I'd just fall from the sky, dribble down a windowpane, swoosh down a drain and run off out to sea. I wouldn't have to worry about making important things happen because I wouldn't have a brain. I'd be a brain without the B, which means I'd just have to go with the flow. I'd just have to trust that I'd make it to the sea. But trusting takes too long. I'm going to *make* things happen *soon*.

At the next bus stop Tory Halligan and her flock of parrots get on. They huddle together, laughing and giggling. Jess bobs up, bounces over and points Tory Halligan to an empty seat near hers.

"Hello," Tory smiles, as she passes me. "The Lieutenant Colonel's daughter." She stands up straight and salutes me, then spins round to salute Jess.

My face starts to burn. Jess bobs back down in her seat.

"H – Hi!" I stammer.

"Interesting hat you're wearing today, Jemima," she says. "Your wardrobe is always such a delight."

My hand slides up to my dad's green beret. If only she knew I had a gas mask in my bag. I know deep down that it's a stupid thing to have, but I can't help the fact that I like it.

Sameena rests her hand on Tory's arm.

"Ssh, Tory," she says. "Give them a break. You know, their dads have just gone, and—"

"I'm not doing anything!" shrieks Tory, breathing Coco Pop breath all over me. "I'm just saying that I like her hat and it's true, I do. Nothing wrong with that! I've decided to do my end of term presentation on fashion and I was thinking I might get some advice from Jemima, that's all."

I keep my eyes fixed on the floor, on the little blob of bubblegum that's greyed out with mud. I will my face to cool down.

"You're such a loveable freak, Jemima," she grins.

Sameena sends me a little smile. Hayley and Beth crowd round, squawking like bright parrots. Pecking for crumbs. They all want to be close to her. They all want to *be* her. Tory salutes me again and leads the fluttering birds towards the back of the bus. Jess bobs up and slides closer to Tory.

"I'm thinking of having a sleepover," she says. "Would you all like to come?"

When you're an army brat like Jess and me you have one of two choices. You choose to fit in or you choose to fit out. Jess took the fitting-in route. I took the fitting out. She likes her life to keep changing. I like mine to stay the same. She likes sucking up to people to get friends. I don't. She gives them things like sweets and treats and sleepovers and does all sorts of stuff she doesn't really want to do, and I won't. Some days I spy on her and sometimes I see her cry. She pretends that she's OK with her life and her dad being away and everything, but I know she's not, not really. I can tell she's hurting behind her big brave smile, just like the rest of us. The problem with Jess is she tries too hard to be liked.

I made my choice years ago when I'd already lived in five different houses, in three different countries and been to four different schools. At my first school I did used to try. I was really young then. I'd stand in the playground and hover on the fringes of the little gangs of girls. Smiling. Hoping. Wondering how to knit myself in. But when I got to my third school and discovered the truth, I gave up. I discovered trying was a pointless waste of time because the army can treat my family like carrots. They can uproot us any time they like and ship us off to the other side of the world. I discovered that fighting wars is more important to the army than caring about girls like me making friends.

I'd wish I could stand on a chair with a megaphone and say to my family, LOOK AT MY LIFE! IT'S NO WONDER I'M FEELING UNHINGED!

What makes matters worse is that I *should* be at boarding school because some bossy body said that boarding school is what happens when you're the daughter of a Lieutenant Colonel. It's supposed to be more settling for army kids. But how can you ever get settled and learn stuff like equations and be interested in Shakespeare or William Blake when your dad is on the other side of the planet with bombs going off around his head? How can you get settled when you're worrying your dad might be lying hurt somewhere? Or that he might even be dead?

I did try boarding once, but I ran away three times and said I would never stop running. And I meant it. When my dad looked into my eyes, he knew I was telling the truth. He said I could stay home until it's time for GCSEs. Then I'll *have* to board. No choice.

I would like to stand on a chair with a megaphone and say, WE'LL SEE ABOUT THAT! But I never want to upset my dad so I swallow down my words.

If my dad didn't have a job that moves us around the world every five minutes and leads him to the edge of death every day, things might be a bit better. I might be able to screw myself back on my hinge.

Chapter 6

I'm not a puddleduck, OK?

I hate school lunchtime more than I hate the bus. The toilets are torture chambers full of bitchy girls like Tory Halligan and the cooks and supervisors are worse. They're the school's sergeant majors. You can see their tonsils dangling when they shout out their commands, and little bubbles of spit that gather in the corners of their mouths when they speak.

"Jemima Taylor-Jones!" shouts Mrs Currie, the head cook. "Uniform!"

I look at her, then down at my boots and smile.

"My dog ate my shoes, miss," I lie. "It was these or my trainers. Mummy thought black was best."

She flaps her bingo wings.

"I was referring to the beret, Jemima," she spits. "This isn't French week, you know! Take it off now, please, before I'm forced to send you to Mrs Bostock's office. And she will confiscate it! Rules are put in place to be adhered to."

"Rules are made to be broken," sniggers Jess, sliding on to the seat next to me. "Have you heard?" she says.

"What?"

"The news?" She pulls out her phone and opens a text from her mum. "There's been *another* bomb," she says. "*Really* bad! Soldiers have been killed. My mum's at home, just waiting for more news. You never know… but then the lines are probably down – we might not find out who's dead for days. It feels weird, knowing it might be my dad. The thought kind of bubbles in my tummy."

She dips a chip in ketchup.

"It's exciting though!" she says. "And us families on the home front are, like, a part of it."

Jess's eyes shimmer. My heart pounds. I shout, SHUT UP, JESS, in my head and hope it's not today my dad gets bombed. I hope it's not today I don't have a dad any more.

I touch the place on my cheek where I hoped his kiss would bloom.

"I've got to go," I say, jumping up and throwing my food in the slop bin.

I run to the quiet area and call my mum.

"Mum!" I say, when she finally answers her phone. "What's happened? Is Dad OK? Jess told me about the bomb."

Mum sighs.

"I wish Georgie would learn to keep that kind of information to herself. It's not helpful Jess knowing all the details. She just blows it out of proportion and gets you all upset. I don't know what's going on, Mima. Yes, there has been a bomb and yes, some people are hurt, but that's all we know so far. You mustn't worry yourself, sweetheart. Try to put it out of your mind and have fun at school. I'll see you later, OK?"

I'm curious at how my mum expects me to have fun at school when I'm so worried all the time that my own dad is in danger. But then I'm curious about so many things.

The lyrics of Kiss Twist's song spin in my mind. I must make my Bring Dad Home mission work. I just have to find a way.

I go to the library looking for inspiration and to find some books on the Blitz. We did it in year five but I need to find out more. I need to work out exactly what happened to Derek and squeeze more information from Granny. Without the facts I won't have a presentation.

"Hi," says Ned Cotsford, looking up from his book.

I blush. My face opens like a bright red rose. I ignore him and start searching along the shelves.

"At this point you're supposed to say, 'Hi, Ned...'"

"Hi," I mumble, turning away.

"Jemima Puddleduck," he smiles, nodding his halo of curly blond hair. "What's up?"

"Nothing's up," I snap. "Leave me alone, will you? I'm busy."

"Sorry," he smiles. "I didn't mean to upset you, Jemima Puddleduck. Just being friendly."

"You didn't upset me," I say. "I just don't want to talk, and I'm not a puddleduck, OK?"

"Ssssshhhhhh," says Mrs Gomez, the librarian. "Jemima, Ned, you're disturbing the peace. This is a quiet zone, remember? For study!"

I glare at her. I don't care about Mrs Gomez being disturbed. She should try living in my body for a day.

Then she'd know all about being disturbed – and unhinged! I bet her dad isn't a million miles away, across the other side of the world. In danger! When she turns back to her work I make a face at her. Stupid Mrs Gomez, what does she know about anything!

Ned laughs, tips his chair back and stretches his legs out in front of him. His eyes burn a hole in my back; they scorch my blazer with flames.

"What you looking for?" he asks, getting up.

"Nothing," I say.

"Not true."

"No, Ned," I say, spinning round to face him. "It's *not* true. But what I'm looking for is none of your business, OK? What I'd really like is for you to leave me alone now. Like Mrs Gomez says, this is a quiet area. For study! And I am trying to study."

I turn back to the books.

Ned gets up. He stands behind me. His breath is on my neck. He peers at the books over my shoulder. He whispers into my ear.

"What are you looking at war books for?" he says. "My gramps was little during the Second World War and he loved it. He says it was exciting watching the Blitz light up the sky like a mega-firework and fun being down in the Anderson shelter waiting for the bombs. He used to run out after the raids and collect bits of old shrapnel and play swapsies with his friends. He's even still got his gas mask and stuff like that. He collects all sorts of war memorabilia, like medals and things. I suppose he's a bit obsessed with it all really. Stuck back in the day. Once he met a German pilot who had crashed down a few streets along. He said it was weird. Seeing the enemy so close and yet him looking like a normal person, the same as everyone else. He said he looked tired and hungry and scared of all us English. Scared of what we might do to him. I think war's stupid. I mean, we're all just people at the end of the day. Why can't we all be friends? What are we fighting for?"

The film images explode in my eyes. "Well, I'm sorry, but your gramps must be mad," I snap. "He obviously didn't lose anyone special in the Blitz. My granny lost her home and everyone she loved all in one day because of stupid bombs. She was left like a little piece of shrapnel in a pile of rubble! There's nothing great or exciting or collectable about that. That's *why* I'm looking for books. I've decided to do my presentation about my granny and this long-lost love of hers, called Derek. The Blitz snatched him away from her. He was going off on a ship and then, like magic, he disappeared. I'm going to find him. For *her*."

"Whoa, sorry, that is serious," Ned says. "But you don't need to bite my head off, Miss Puddleduck. Just because my gramps is into war it doesn't mean that I am. I'm not a sheep, you know, who just follows along. I'm a person with thoughts and feelings of my own. In fact, if you're really interested to know, I'm a pacifist."

"What's a pacifist?" I ask. His halo hair glints in the sun.

"Someone who doesn't believe in war or violence at all," he says. "I believe governments should learn to talk to each other instead of sending their countries to war. Violence doesn't help anyone. Peace is the way forward. I promise you." His eyes sparkle. "Your dad's in the army, isn't he?"

I nod.

"He's mad. Why risk your life? What for?"

"I won't ask you two again," hisses Mrs Gomez. "BE QUIET!"

Ned sits down and picks up his book. I turn back to the shelves.

My brain buzzes. Why *does* my dad risk his life? Why is he so obsessed? He's as crazy as Ned's gramps. They'd probably get on well. I pull a book off the shelf and slide down to the floor. I open it and rest it on my knees and pretend to read. Then I think about some of the reasons my dad goes to war and my eyes start swimming with tears. My tummy twists up in knots.

"My dad goes to war," I whisper, "because the army is in his bones. Because he's protecting our country. Because he believes it's the right thing to do. Because it's his way of earning money to feed me and Milo and Mum."

And that feels scary. My dad risks his *life* to put food in my tummy, which means every little cell of me has grown from money from war. Every little breath, every mouthful of food, every jumper and pair of jeans, every dress and coat. My cot. My bed. My curtains. My walls. My toys. My school bag. My necklace. My magazines. Everything in my life has been paid for by war. Yuck.

"Dad," I whisper to the shelves, "you're so stupid! You

don't have to risk your life, you dummy! Why can't you do something else? You could be a potter, for instance, or a banker or a judge. You could drive cars or make bread. But don't risk your life to feed me. Please!"

Then Granny's words scuttle through my head. *It's in his bones!*

Well, I wish it wasn't in his bones!

"And then you have to consider the other side of it," Ned whispers. "Like the fact that he probably has to *kill* people, Jemima Puddleduck. Serious things like that. You know, *their* blood is on *his* hands."

My breath catches in my throat. I've only ever worried about my dad being killed. I've never even considered the fact that he might have to kill someone else, that my own dad might be a murderer. I imagine him standing face to face, eye to eye, with someone he's about to kill. And that person might have a daughter, like me, back home, who is scared of the wind, scared of end of term presentations, scared of everything. Worried that her dad might die.

I stroke an angel on my arm and whisper silently to the sky, "Please come home."

I turn to Ned.

"I am *trying* to get him home," I say. "I am *trying* to stop him. I'd do anything to bring him back."

I'd do *anything* to bring him home.

"Does being a pacifist mean you wouldn't ever fight back, Ned?" I ask. "You know, if I punched you in the face right now or if someone came and tried to kill you and all your family. Would you just sit there and do nothing?"

"Mmmmm, good point," smiles Ned. "Except I haven't really got a family. It's just Gramps and me. But anyway, try me?"

"I'm not going to hit you," I say. "I just wondered, you know, what if? Like there must be *some* kind of war you might fight? Something you might stand up for? Something you might do?"

"Maybe. But that's the point. If *everyone* were a pacifist there'd be no wars to fight. Everyone would live in peace. How amazing would that be? That's what John Lennon was talking about."

"John Lennon?" I ask. "Who's he?"

"John Lennon? Oh, he's no one really," he sighs. "Just one of the greatest legends the world has ever known. Have you been hiding in a box all your life,

Jemima Puddleduck, or under the stairs like Harry Potter? Haven't you heard the song?"

Then he quietly sings a bit of it to me and it's all about imagining that there was nothing to fight about or have wars for, imagining that all the people in the world could live in peace.

Ned has a voice like an angel that gently soothes my heart. I close my eyes and start imagining and I really get what he's singing about.

"That kind of peace *would* be amazing," I say, "and that's what I want too. I'm sure most people do. But before the earth is overflowing and full of peace is there anything you'd fight for? I mean, would you fight for peace or just sit around hoping?"

"I'll have to think on that one," he says. "I'd maybe do a peaceful protest or something. But there must be other ways of creating peace, you know – being kind to people, helping when you can, that kind of thing."

"That all sounds lovely, Ned," I say, rushing to get my books scanned and stamped and pushing my way out of the big library doors, "but I haven't got time to wait and be peaceful. I need to fight to get my dad back. Now, before it's too late."

"Wait up," calls Ned, running at my side. "What's going on? You're acting super-weird, Jemima Puddleduck."

"Just leave me alone, Ned," I say. "There's stuff I have to do, OK?"

But he won't go. He's an irritating wasp buzzing around my ear.

"What stuff?" he asks. "Can I come too? I can help you get your dad back and find the long-lost love."

I spin to face him.

"No, Ned, please! I'm serious. Just leave me alone."

I hurry to the science block. I can't wait any longer. If I'm going to get my dad home I have to turn up the heat. I have to get him home before he gets killed and before he kills anyone else. No one needs to die. It's stupid. I *will* stop this.

I scan the corridor. It's quiet. My legs turn to jelly and a sickly chill creeps under my skin. I've never done anything like this before. I've never been so bad.

My life has become a war zone. I pull my dad's beret from my blazer pocket and put it on. I imagine my gas mask over my face and I'm marching with the battalion, a real part of a real war. I'm marching and marching in my twinkling black boots. My dad is beside me, smiling. He salutes me like the soldier who collected him from home and I salute him back. Lieutenant Colonel Taylor-Jones! I do want peace in this world, but I want my dad home more. I'm not like Ned. I'm not going to sit around waiting for six months. I'm like my dad and I will fight...

I scan the corridor for danger, checking for the enemy. My heart is an angel in my chest. Flapping hard to be free.

Then I press my thumb on the fire-alarm glass until it cracks and fills the school with its urgent bell.

Chapter 7

I turn to the window and stare out at the rain...

On Tuesday morning I creep into Dad's wardrobe to fill my nose with his smell again. I put his beret back on the shelf and pull down a cap with a golden badge on the front. I tip tap and rap rap my fist along the back wall of the wardrobe, looking for a secret door to another glorious world, like Lucy from *The Lion, the Witch and the Wardrobe*. It would be amazing if I found one. I mean, if I actually fell out into another place full of interesting things to see. Somewhere secret, that no one else would ever know about. If I were still six I might even make up a game that it did actually happen and I might dress up like Lucy and get some stuffed toys to be like Mr Tumnus and all the other people in the book. But I'm twelve and twelve is confusing, so I won't. And anyway, I'm in the real world where nothing brilliant like that ever happens.

Before I leave the house I send an e-bluey to my dad.

Dear Dad,

Have you ever thought of doing a different job? I was thinking you might like to be a potter or a baker? Then you wouldn't have to go away all the time. I like it better when you're here. I feel safer. We all do. But Granny says the army is in your bones. Is that true?

I've decided to do my end of term presentation on Granny and the Blitz. Do you know anything about what happened to her? And have you even heard anything about Derek, her long-lost love? I've got some books from the library, but I'm not doing very well with my research. I want to try to find him for her. It's so sad what happened to her, Dad.

Please write back soon if you have any information.

I love you and miss you a million trillion and wish
you weren't so far away,

Mima xxx

PS I'm scared that you kill people. Do you?

*   *   *

At lunchtime it's time for the next part of my Bring Dad
Home mission. I creep into the art block. It's quiet
and dark and all the wonderful smells of paint and clay and
glue still linger in the air. The corridor is full of amazing
paintings, brilliant colours shining through the gloom.

I put Dad's cap on and imagine myself stamping my
big black boots in time with the march. Keeping up
with the battalion, saluting my dad, Lieutenant Colonel
Taylor-Jones.

I check the corridor one last time for the enemy.

The angel in my chest beats its wings hard, flapping
and flapping with fear.

I put my thumb on the fire-alarm glass and press and
press until it cracks.

The shrill bell shatters the air and sends everyone flying.
We race from the building and bundle into the playground.
We wait in our fire-drill lines while teachers walk up and
down and call out our names. Checking the register,

78

making sure we're safe. The fire brigade pile through the gates. Blue lights are flashing. A smile creeps on my lips.

When the fire brigade are certain there's no real fire, we're sent back to our classrooms. Mrs Bostock is fuming. Her cheeks are much hotter than flames. She struts up and down the playground, tutting. She scans the crowd with her beady eyes.

"Whoever here is responsible for this time-wasting nuisance," she says, "you be sure that I will find you!"

Her eyes fly over me and land on Tory Halligan.

I've never walked around with such a secret before. Something so big that no one else knows, something so terribly, terribly bad.

"Who d'you think it is?" says Jess, bobbing about on the bus seat on our way home. "Did you see Mrs Bostock's eyes when the fire brigade were leaving? She was so furious they were almost popping out of her head."

I turn to the window. I stare out at the rain and smile.

On Wednesday morning I don't want to get out of bed. We've still heard nothing from my dad. He hasn't replied to my e-bluey, he hasn't phoned and so far no one's told us that he's dead.

"When something bad happens over there," says Mum, pulling up my blind, "they turn all communications off in case things leak out to the press. They have to get their facts right first. Then they tell the families and write their reports. We won't hear from him, sweetheart, until all that's done. But I'm sure he's fine, Mima. If he weren't, I think someone would have told us by now. Come on. Up now! And off to school. Don't let it get to you."

Mum is so big with the baby she doesn't feel like my mum any more. Her tummy is a huge round egg. I wonder when this baby will hatch.

After lunch I creep into the music department. The orchestra is practising in the hall. I peep through the window and see Mr Denergri. He's the conductor and his arms are flailing wildly. His straw-coloured hair has flopped into his eyes. His conducting baton is drawing beautiful patterns in the air and the music is rising like doves. The orchestra is concentrating hard and I'm concentrating on my Bring Dad Home mission. We all have a job to do, but if mine is going to work, I need to turn up the heat. Mrs Bostock needs to fry.

The angel in my chest flaps a feeble beat. So scared, its wings tremble, more frightened than I am of the wind.

Without bothering to check for the enemy, without bothering to march with my dad, I press my thumb into the glass. The shrieking bell spreads through the school like wildfire.

Mrs Bostock is beyond angry. She's more than fuming. She's about to burst.

"This behaviour is unacceptable!" she spits. "I will not have this kind of disruption in my school!"

I rub my tummy, the place where my secret lives.

"I'm offended," huffs Tory Halligan on the way back home on the bus. "Mrs Bostock had the audacity to drag *me* into her office and accuse *me* of setting off the alarm. Why me? What have I ever done to anyone? My dad's going to have something to say about this."

When I get home I can't settle to anything. I try to squeeze more information about Derek out of Granny but her mouth is zipped shut.

"Not now, pet," she says, pulling wet sheets out of the washing machine. "Not now."

Mum can't stop cleaning.

"I think the baby's coming soon," she smiles. "Looks like I'm nesting!" She strokes my cheek. "I wish your dad was here," she says. "He should be with us at a time like this."

I wish I could stand on the kitchen table and shout through a megaphone, I AM TRYING, MUM, I REALLY AM! I'M TRYING TO BRING HIM BACK HOME! But I don't. Instead I make Granny and Mum a nice cup of tea and help them clean out the kitchen cupboards. But I can't see the point, really; they'll only get dirty again.

As soon as I go up to bed I hear Mum switch on the news. I think about the Bean swimming about in its secret world inside her and about Mum giving birth without Dad. Life is so unfair sometimes. Why can't it be fairer? Who makes things happen how they do? I can hear the news banging and crashing over the screen and I know Mum's damp hanky will be all twisted in her hands.

I'm in and out of sleep, hot and sweaty under my duvet. Big baby faces loom in the dark, laughing and gurgling. Blood from Dad's war films keeps bothering my eyes and I'm just about to drift off again when Jess sends another text.

Pip. Pip. *There's been another 1. A suicide bomber this time. What if it's one of our dads?! We had another takeaway for tea. U OK?*

I switch off my phone and throw it in my bag. I'm trying to remember Dad's face, but my mind is like butter. He keeps slipping away, disappearing into the blackness of the night. I try to remember our farewell party. I can see Uncle Michael and Dad's friend Phil, but Dad's completely covered in barbecue smoke. It's following him, hiding him, smudging him over. I can see his boots and I can see his kit, but I can't see him. Then everything goes up in flames and the school fire alarm shrieks through my head and deafens my ears. The entire school is crushed into the hall with Mrs Bostock's voice booming. Jess is smiling. She hopes her dad is dead and Tory Halligan has turned into a bird.

I wake up out of breath with dreaming. It's dark. I climb out of bed, creep across the landing and slide into Granny's room. She's still awake, sipping hot chocolate and having a go at the crossword.

"Hello, pet," she says, pulling back the cover. "Want to slip in?"

"Please tell me a story, Granny," I say, settling into her

nest. "Tell me about Derek and the Blitz and everything. I really need to know. I'm doing it for my presentation, like you suggested, and I've been looking at books and everything, but it's not the same as hearing it from you."

"You're just like your dad," she smiles, offering me a sip of her drink. "You never give up, do you? I'm not sure there's much to say, really. There's so much I don't remember any more."

"Try, Granny, try. Pleeeeaaasssee?"

And I wish and I wish she'd give in.

"Well…" she says, "when I was small we used to go to Bognor Regis. Every year we'd pack our bags and off we'd go. Then when I was about four we met Derek and his family on the beach. They say you can't fall in love so young, but I knew he was special in an instant." She picks up the photo of him from her bedside table and kisses his face. "I couldn't resist those eyes, see; well, who could? Then year after year, same place, same fortnight, we were inseparable. True friends we were. Kindred spirits, you might say. And who knows what might have happened if the course of history had changed. But like I said before, if I'd married Derek then I wouldn't have had Daddy and Daddy wouldn't have had you. And I wouldn't want to be without you, Mima. Life works out, you know, you just have to trust."

"I don't like trusting," I say. "It scares me."

"Well, trusting is the only thing that got me through," she sighs. "The Blitz rained on London like a storm and everyone's lives were turned upside down." Her eyes fill and sparkle with tears. "All us kids that hadn't been evacuated already were at school and the rest of my family was home. Then there was a daytime raid one time, see, and we hid in the shelter. Watching. Listening. Waiting. We held our breath. Waiting to see where the bombs would land."

Granny stops talking. Her eyes look right through me, searching for ghosts in the past. I take another sip of her drink.

"Bombs all around," she says. "Rubble and shrapnel everywhere. Rooms exploded wide open. Like film sets with pictures left on the walls. Flower vases toppled on the shelves. Furniture left in the rain, waiting for people who never came home. Except me, that is. I did come home... but I was the only one; they'd all gone, see, every one of them. I was numb with fury for a while. I scrabbled through the mess. Searched for them all, looked for fragments, looked for anything that was left of my family, anything that was left of my life."

I fold Granny's paper-thin hand in mine.

"That's when I found the photos, see," she says, "and all the bits in the box. That's all that was left. Then someone picked me up like an insect off a leaf and carried me away. And that was that, the end of the first chapter of my life. Then I was evacuated to Wales, with that box full of bits in my hand and a thousand questions racing around my mind."

"Were you scared, Granny?" I whisper.

"I was quaking in my boots," she says. "And if I hadn't learned to trust life I would've driven myself crazy trying to change what happened. But we can't change something once it's done. We can't take words back, as much as we'd like to, Mima, as much as we'd like to try to rearrange it all in our mind. You can't resist what's so. Life is a mysterious thing and we can't control it, however hard we try."

She sighs. Her hand trembles in mine.

"Trying to control life," she says, "is like trying to stop the waves."

"And Derek?" I ask. "What happened to him?"

"I can't answer that, see," she says. "The last thing I

86

heard was he and his family were off on some ship to Canada, some great adventure. He said he'd write. But I was gone; I was in Wales. I couldn't find his address in the rubble so there was nothing more I could do. Over the years I've got used to the fact that I'll never know if he wrote to me or not. I've been to Bognor Regis looking a few times, but I never found him. I couldn't remember where he lived. I was so young and in so much shock." She laughs. "My dotty old memory. The whole thing's a bit silly, really; just sweethearts we were, that's all."

"What was his second name?" I ask. "Do you remember that?"

"Oh, I don't know, pet," she says. "I think it was Bach; something like that, anyway. But I had to get on, see, and then I met your grandpa and I tried to leave it all behind."

"And what about Grandpa?" I ask. "Does Derek mean you didn't really love him?"

"Of course I loved your grandpa, pet," she says, stroking my face. "Derek was different, that's all. Someone I'll always treasure in my memory and never ever forget."

Chapter 8

Someone tries the door handle...

On Thursday morning I creep into Dad's wardrobe. I stand in front of his scarlet mess dress jacket and wrap his empty ghost arms round me. I close my eyes and he's here, in scarlet and gold and black shiny shoes, holding me tight. I remember the last time he wore it. They were going to some special evening at the mess. Mum had a beautiful black dress on and smelled like a flower and Dad was all dressed up in this. Milo and me were in our pyjamas, eating popcorn and watching a film and Dad sat between us and pulled us on to his lap.

"You two," he smiled, "better get to bed soon because

there's pancakes to be made in the morning! So quick march, Major Milo! You first!"

And Milo squealed and squirrelled and bashed Dad with his legs until Dad swung him high in the air and flew him straight to bed. And we all laughed and Dad whispered that I was allowed to stay up later than late with Clea, our babysitter, and Milo never found out.

I rub my face in the cloth and get a noseful of his smell, then pull back my sleeves and set a million angels free. They rise from my arms, a flash of pure brilliance. Snow-white wings soaring high into the sky towards the scorching sun.

At lunchtime the air in the dining hall is stretched so tight I think it might pop. The angel in my chest flaps. Everyone is waiting. Waiting. Waiting. Like me waiting for my dad.

"D'you think it'll happen again?" asks Ned, tucking into his pie. "I mean, it can't go on for ever, can it? Eventually someone's going to be caught. I think they should start fingerprinting – that would sort things out."

"Oh, Neddy," says Tory Halligan, sliding in next to him. "It's not fair. Can you believe that Mrs Bostock accused me? I mean, why would she? What have I ever done to make her think such a thing? I'm going to stick with you this lunchtime, Neddy – you can be my alibi."

"Whoever it is," says Jess, "they're in big trouble. Did you see Mrs Bostock's face? What d'you think will happen when she finds them? D'you think they'll get expelled?"

I smile.

"I'm sure they will," I say.

My hand finds the box of matches in my pocket. I turn them over. I rub my thumb over the rough bit that sets the match on fire. I smile. My dad will come home soon. I'm sure of it now.

When we leave the dining hall, the teachers are all over the school. Walking up and down with beady eyes. Watching. Waiting. Listening for the alarm.

I slide away from the others and creep to the science block. Strong chemical smells bite my nose. Sting my eyes. Stick in my throat. My hands tremble, my neck is sticky with sweat. The angel beats and beats its wings. I drag a stool to the bench and pull out the matches. I strike one and watch the bright yellow blaze creep up the little stick until it nips my fingers. I turn the Bunsen burner on then off. Off then on, freeing the hissing gas. Ppppsssssssss! Pppppppppsssssss!

I pull Dad's scarlet mess dress jacket out of my bag and slip it on. I need him here with me today. The gold brocade glints in the sunlight, sending rainbow fairies spinning around the room. I stroke the matchbox. I think. I free some more hissing gas. On and off. Off and on. Ppppppssssssss! Ppppppsssssssss! I think some more. And I may feel powerful and brave right now, but I'm not stupid. I am a Taylor-Jones, after all!

I turn the gas off.

I put the matches in my pocket and slide off the stool. I go out into the corridor and smash my thumb into the glass. The angel thump thump thumps, drumming a way out of my chest. I hop back into the science lab, slam the door and push a chair against the handle. My breath is coming in thick and lumpy gasps. I'm dizzy. The shrill alarm screeches through my head. Drills into my brain and a thousand footsteps thunder through the school. There are skids and squeals and whoops. Doors slam. Chairs scrape. Everyone races to the playground. Fire engines flash whirling blue shadows across the walls.

I stack some stools and tables against the door to

barricade myself in and tuck myself under Mrs Fox's desk. I strike another match and watch it creep along the stick until it runs out of wood and nips me. Ouch!

Someone tries the door handle. I freeze. They push and push until it opens a crack.

"Who's in there?" demands a man with a deep voice. "Are you OK?"

I keep really still. He tries again. Thud. Thud. Thud. I hear him whisper to someone else.

"Something's up," he says. "There's no smoke, but something's not right." He raises his voice again so I can hear. "Don't panic," he shouts. "I'm coming in. If you're hurt, lie still."

He's the one panicking. I'm OK! He shakes the handle and pushes hard, making the stack of tables and stools creak across the floor. The door rattles and thuds and the tables and chairs inch further and further in.

I'm silent because I'm not really here. I'm dust in the crack in the floor.

"Excuse me…" shouts the voice. "We're looking for Jemima Taylor-Jones, so if it's you in there, Jemima, you need to let me know. If you can't speak, bang something. OK?"

I shrink even more. I am smaller than a mouse, tinier than a spider, teenier than a flea. I need to wait until Mrs Bostock is cooked, until she's baked to a burn.

With one last push the man throws himself at the door, sending the stools toppling like skittles. He heaves his shoulder into the load, screeching the tangle of legs across the polished wooden floor. When the gap is big enough he pops through like a champagne cork and two more firemen bubble in behind. They don't see me at first and I enjoy the worried look in their eyes, and it's not until Mrs Bostock pops in and dumps her big red bag on the desk that anyone notices where I am.

While the firemen check the room for fire, she looks under the desk.

"Jemima!" she squeaks. "What on earth are you doing under Mrs Fox's desk? What in heaven's name is going on? You're not the one causing all this trouble and setting off the alarms, are you?"

I stare at the floor. The back of my neck is sticky with heat.

"Jemima!" she squawks. "Will you answer my question, please? Are you or are you not responsible for the alarms?"

I turn the matches in my hand. I rattle them in their box.

"It *is* you, isn't it?" she says. "I'm utterly shocked, Jemima! I wouldn't have thought for a moment that you... I... Why?"

Mrs Bostock apologises profusely to the firemen.

"It's a darned nuisance," one of them gruffs. "Kids playing about like that."

He peers under the table at me.

"D'you hear me?" he says. "Types like you are a nuisance to society. A waste of taxpayers' money."

Mrs Bostock promises our school won't trouble the fire brigade again and sends them away. Then she turns to me.

"Jemima," she says, "explain to me exactly what's going on."

I shake my head and shrink back. I'm not here. I'm dust in the crack. Mrs Bostock sighs and drums her fingers on the desk. She brushes invisible dust from her skirt. She counts to ten.

"I'm going to leave this room," she snaps, "send everyone back to their classrooms, and then meet you in my office in five minutes. And I warn you, Jemima,

94

my patience is wearing thin. No messing around. Understand?"

I nod. I try to smile.

And now I'm in Mrs Bostock's office, watching a Blitz explode behind her sparkling blue eyes.

"I order you to tell me exactly what is going on," she snaps. "Just what were you trying to prove, Jemima?"

I shake my head. I'm not going to tell her anything. If my plan is going to work I need to stretch her until she snaps.

"I can't talk to you properly, Jemima," she says, "unless you tell me what's going on. Did someone put you up to it? Is that it? Were you bullied into setting off the alarms? Because if that's the case you must tell me! Now! I won't have *that* kind of behaviour in my school. Bullying will not be tolerated."

I shake my head.

"So if it's not bullying then," she says, "what happened? Of all the people in this school you're the last person I'd have imagined to do this kind of thing. You're usually such a little mouse."

She paces up and down the room with her arms

folded across her chest. An angry little vein drums in her neck.

I want to stand on her big red leather chair and shout, IN ACTUAL FACT, MRS BOSTOCK, I AM NOT A MOUSE. I MIGHT LOOK LIKE THAT FROM THE OUTSIDE BECAUSE MY WORDS GET CLOGGED IN MY THROAT, BUT ACTUALLY I'M A LION! And then I'd like to eat her up and go home and make popcorn with Milo.

"So if you did do it," she says, "what I can't work out is why? What benefit is there in setting off fire alarms and making a nuisance of yourself? And you're such a nice girl, Jemima. I can't make it out. Something just doesn't add up."

I shrug. I'll show her I'm not really a mouse. I'll show Mum I'm not unhinged!

I shove Dad's mess dress jacket sleeves high up my arms and watch her eyes shriek as loud as the fire alarm when they land on the inky angels on my skin. She zips her mouth. The red island stain bleeds on to her face. I smile.

"Is it because of Dad?' she asks, watching me flick the sliver of nail I just tore from my finger land on her precious carpet. "Are you missing him or is it Mummy having the baby? Has someone upset you, Jemima? Because, you see, as far as my experience tells, people don't usually make trouble for no reason. Generally they're upset about something and their behaviour is a cry for help."

Using the sharp edge of my remaining fingernail, I burrow a little hole in my tights and stretch it hard so a nylon ladder snakes its way down my leg. Mrs Bostock's eyes dart from the nail to the ladder to my inky arms and back again. I'm mixing her brain in a blender. Whizzing her up into soup. If I keep being difficult I *will* get what I want. She *will* expel me. She'll be left with no choice. Then she'll call my mum and my mum will call my dad and then the army will *have* to send him home.

Having a problem child who plays with fire *must* be a bad enough thing.

I take a deep breath. I smile.

Mrs Bostock sighs. She rubs her hands together. She clip clops round her desk on her thin spiky heels and comes so close to me that her large doughy breasts jiggle under my nose.

"I have been head teacher of Summerbrooks for over twenty-five years," she smiles. "And believe you me, Jemima, I've seen every trick in the book. Truanting, cheating, bullying, bubblegum, lipstick, defiance, destruction, ladders in tights, bitten nails, drawings on arms, big black boots, jewellery and lies. I haven't, I must confess, seen such beautiful jackets worn in place of blazers, but apart from that I've seen the lot. And you may think you're so very daring and that I'm about to snap in half and have a tantrum, but I promise you, Jemima, I'm made of stronger stuff than that."

The angel in my chest drops its wings and dies. It's over. I'm lost.

She totters over to the sofa, sits down and beckons me to join her. The red island stain drains away. The shrieking alarms melt in her eyes.

"The thing is, Jemima, I'm on your side. I'm your friend. I'm here to listen. So tell me what the problem is and let's see how I can help. Or if you think you'd prefer to talk to a professional counsellor…"

"Aren't you going to expel me?" I ask. "And call my mum?"

Mrs Bostock smiles.

"And what good would that do?" she says. "What you need, Jemima, is help, not rejection. In all my years as head teacher, I have never felt the need to expel a soul. So I'm not about to start now."

She takes hold of my hand. An annoying little muscle starts twitching in my eye.

"I'm committed to helping you, Jemima." She pulls a huge tin from the shelf and offers me a chocolate. "Now, tell me what's up. What's eating you?"

I put the chocolate in my mouth and stare at the floor.

"Nothing…" I say. "I just… I need…"

Blue flashing fire-engine lights whirl in front of my eyes. Clattering and skidding and shrieking alarm bells drill into my ears. Everybody's time! All this trouble! What would my dad say if he knew what I've done? A handful of sharp-edged diamonds well up and sting my eyes. My dad wouldn't be proud of this. He wouldn't be proud of me creating all this trouble.

I swallow the lump in my throat. Suddenly I feel quite small. She's right. Mum's right. I turn back into an unhinged mouse.

"I'm sorry, Mrs Bostock," I say. "I didn't mean…

well, I did mean... but I'm sorry. I won't do it again. I promise."

"Let's keep this to ourselves, shall we?" she smiles, patting my hand. "Mum's got enough to worry about without us making things worse. I'm not condoning your behaviour, Jemima. You've caused a lot of trouble and wasted a lot of time and that's unacceptable. But I trust that now you know I'm on your side you'll be able to come to me with your worries. Never forget, help is at hand. A problem shared and all that. But rules are rules. I will be keeping an eye on you, Jemima. I'll be collecting reports from your teachers every week and I'd like you to pay me a visit after lunch each day for a little chat. Just you and me. To air your problems."

She slips a fistful of chocolates in my pocket.

"Off you trot now," she smiles. "Back to class."

Chapter 9

I kick the back of the wardrobe...

It's Saturday and the wind is up again. It whistles around the house. Bangs on the windows. Rips through the trees. I climb into Dad's wardrobe. I feel safe in here. Close to his clothes. Close to his smell. Three weeks have passed and we still haven't heard a thing. Every time the phone rings my ears stretch out for his voice. But it's always Georgie or one of the other officers' wives calling to arrange coffee mornings and shopping trips. Georgie keeps coming over for yoga and breathing practice in preparation for being Mum's birthing partner when the Bean decides to hatch. I think it's stupid. My dad should be with her, not Georgie.

I'm angry with Mrs Bostock. If she were a normal head teacher she would have expelled me by now. Then my dad would be home and even though he'd be cross with me for being expelled I wouldn't be afraid of the wind. I wouldn't be worried that he's dead. Or scared that he's killed someone else.

I kick the back of the wardrobe. Real life is rubbish. I wish I were a character in a book full of fauns and lions and magical worlds. Even the tyranny of the white witch and permanent frosty winter would be better than this.

Nobody, except Mrs Bostock, knows it was me that set off the fire alarms and my secret is sitting in my tummy, scorching like a blister bubbling and cracking inside. Yesterday, when everyone was talking on the bus home from school Ned said, "I think I know who set off the alarms."

And Jess said, "Who then, clever clogs?"

And Ned said, "I'm not telling."

He turned to me and his eyes drilled into my mine, like he could almost see right through me, right to my secret, hiding inside.

And part of me wanted to tell him, but that would

be too risky, so I kept my gaze steady and my face quite still and I smiled.

"I don't even understand Mrs Bostock wanting to keep it private," Jess carried on. "The alarms disrupted us all. So I think we all deserve to know who did it and what punishment they're going to get. It was a stupid thing to do. My mum said it was really inconsiderate. Not to mention dangerous. And time-wasting. Maybe they got seven hundred hours of extra prep? Or a million trillion lines?"

And I said, "Maybe she's going to have them hung, drawn and quartered in assembly, Jess. Or beheaded, or something worse."

Jess's eyes shone as huge as the moon. And she said, "Let's hope so because I heard that Mrs Bostock's office is like a dungeon. Anyone who gets sent there apparently *never* comes out alive. Maybe she hangs them from the walls on chains and whips them? Maybe she feeds them to the wolves?"

Then Tory Halligan and her parrots fluttered over and she slid down next to Ned and said, "Whoever it was deserves a really bad punishment. I mean, *I* might have been punished for something *I* didn't do. My reputation might have gone downhill."

And I just smiled again and my secret glowed inside.

I take a last big sniff of Dad's jumper, hop out of his wardrobe and slide back to my room. I'm hiding from Mum. She's now gone totally crazy with the baby-nesting cleaning and she keeps nagging me to sort out my room. What I don't understand is why she gives me a room if I can't keep it how I like. I'm not like my mum. I *like* things all over the floor and piled on my chair. I *like* mould growing in my cups and toast crumbs in my bed. I *like* my clothes in a jumble and my books in a heap and my bed in a rumpletuff.

What I *don't* like is straight lines like her.

Straight lines and neat things make me feel like a sandwich living in a lunch box. All tight and wrapped up in foil. All quiet next to an apple and a packet of crisps that aren't allowed to say hello to each other in case someone gets crumpled or bruised.

I'm more like a wilderness. A tangle. A jungle. And if my mum and me were flowers she'd be a straight, straight stem with a pure blue iris on the top. Whereas I'd be a yellow jasmine scattered up the wall.

I open my laptop and Google *The Blitz*. If Mrs Bostock is refusing to expel me, then I have to get on with my research. We have to present our ideas on Monday, which is a perfect day to start part three of my Bring Dad Home mission. I've decided not to cause trouble again because trouble won't make Dad proud. So part three of my plan is all about me.

Google says that the word Blitz means 'Lightning War'. I don't like lightning. I find some paper and draw a picture of a little girl. It's supposed to be Granny when she was nine. She's holding her box and her eyes are huge with shock. Bombs are raining all around. Breaking up the earth. Bringing down the houses. I draw big white jagged cracks of lightning and huge black planes that slice up the sky. On another piece of paper I draw Derek's solemn face and big soft eyes. He's standing by a big ship with his gas mask on and a suitcase in his hand. I draw a big funnel on the ship with plumes of smoke blasting into the air. I draw a fat arrow and write *Canada* inside.

Round each picture I carefully draw a big red heart. I cut them both out and arrange them on the floor. I think I'm going to make a picture board for my presentation and draw hearts and arrows with Granny on one side, Derek on the other. I rummage through Granny's box and find a photo of her when she was about nine and put it next to my drawing. I need a photo of Derek, really, so it's even, but the only one I have of him is hiding in Granny's bra. And there's no point in even asking her for that. I'll have to come up with another plan.

I Google *Derek Bach*. In all my wildest dreams I hope he'll leap off the page, smiling, with roses for Granny and a photo for me in his hand. But real life isn't dreams and I don't get very far. The only Derek Bachs I can find are a footballer that looks too young to have known Granny before the war and a businessman in America, which is too far away to come for a school presentation. And even though America is close to Canada, in my heart I know this man is not him. After that the search only brings up Dereks who play music or the famous classical music composer, Johann Sebastian Bach.

Rubbish.

I dig deeper and deeper into my Blitz search and find out all about air raids and Anderson shelters and evacuation and food rations. Some of the pictures are incredible. One is of a man standing on a pile of rubble, looking so lost and alone and scared. And he's a man. How must that have been for Granny? I have to find a way to make her tell me more. I can't do my presentation without her.

All my research is interesting but I don't want my presentation to be about facts.

I want it to be about love.

I want everyone to see how war shreds people's hearts.

Ned can fight for peace. I'm standing up for love.

I draw a huge red heart. I cut it out and make a zigzag cut down the middle so it looks like a broken heart. I put it between the smaller hearts with my drawings on, then I put the photo of Granny on her side and dig out the one of Derek's sisters for his. They'll have to do for now. I need someone to take me to the shop for some card as sad and grey as the rain. Then I can stick it all on with some sparkles and hearts so Mrs Cassidy can see I've made a start.

Now I'm really excited. The idea of my presentation being about love makes me think about Dad and me. I pull out two more sheets of paper and draw two red hearts. I draw a picture of me in one heart and a picture of Dad in the other. I need to print out some photos so I can stick them on too. Then I draw a million inky angels and some tiny red felt-tip pen hearts. They're exploding out of our chests and travelling off the edge of the page, trying to reach each other. Then I remember my great-grandparents. They were parted by war too. They did actually die. And baby Joan. I draw another heart and put all of them inside.

Granny's box is full of broken hearts.

Ideas for my presentation are filling my body with light that's fizzing and overflowing like stars. Maybe I could do an interview and make a newspaper with photos… or maybe I could even make…

A film!

Something heavy but light at the same time lands in my bones and sparkles like snowflakes on my skin.

I'm so excited. I run to tell Granny.

"Granny," I say, tumbling into the kitchen, "something's landed in my bones. Just like you said."

She laughs. "Told you so, pet. Told you to stop worrying and start trusting what comes. What is it then? Spill the beans!"

"Well," I say, "I think I'd like to be a documentary maker when I grow up. I want to make films about people and life and all the beautiful and wonderful mysteries of the world. I'm going to start with a film for my presentation and then just keep going on from there."

Granny chuckles. Her eyes shimmer in the light.

"And… I was wondering," I say. "Well, I know talking about the Blitz upsets you and everything… but I was wondering whether I could make a film about you, Granny? Talking about the war?"

"We'll see, pet," chuckles Granny, patting a pile of clean washing. "We'll see. A film all about me? Whatever next!"

"And I know I said I didn't want to do the presentation because I get scared talking in front of people," I say, "but I'm so excited now, I don't care about looking silly. I'm just going to stand up and do it anyway."

Inspiration fizzes me faster than a rocket back up the stairs. I grab Dad's camcorder and run to my room for my camera. I have so many plans.

I pull back my sleeves and ink in Dad's fading angels. Then I set them free. A radiant flash of brilliant white wings swoop and soar through the sky. A million angels settle around him. A million angels guard him. A million angels to keep him safe until I can bring him home.

Chapter 10

Just stuff, I say...

It's Sunday and Milo's been playing Action Man since six o'clock this morning. He's turned his bedroom into a camp and he's charging about the house wearing combats, with a Superman cape round his shoulders and a Robin Hood hat on his head.

"Rrrroooaaaaarrrrr," he roars, diving on to my bed. "Rrrroooaaaaarrrrr."

I tickle him.

"Rrrroooooaaaaaarrrrrrr!" I say. "Hey, Milo, fancy dressing up in something else to help me with my presentation? Want to make a film?"

His eyes light up and he drops on his knees and pants

like a dog. I pat his head, pick up Dad's camcorder and my camera and take him back to his room.

"You need to look old-fashioned," I say, "like a schoolboy in the war."

We pull on his school uniform, which is really old-fashioned, and makes him look so cute. He has these long grey socks and shorts that hang to his knees and a grey shirt and a jumper with a V neck. I lace his shoes. I pull on his blazer and slick back his hair with spit.

"Look at you," I say, standing him in front of the mirror. "You look exactly like an evacuee. Just like Derek. I need you for my presentation board, you see."

I pull the gas mask over Milo's face, tie a name tag to his blazer and put the little brown suitcase from the car boot sale in his hand.

"Perfect!" I smile. "Now imagine you're about to go away to Canada. You're going away and you're not going to see me or Mum or Granny or Dad for ages and ages and ages… and the truth is, because it's the war, you might never even see us again."

Milo starts acting all sad.

"That's it," I say. "Brilliant, Milo. When I turn on the camera give me a sad little wave and say, 'Bye-bye!'

And then start crying so much, like your world's about to end. Look really scared because of the bombs thundering all around."

Milo makes a brilliant evacuee. I take a few photos for my picture board, then video him waving goodbye. He looks so lost and cute and scared, and he's just getting into acting it out when Mum crashes her way up the stairs. She barges into Milo's room and erupts like a lightning war.

"Jemima!" she shrieks, yanking the gas mask from Milo's face and stripping off his clothes like they're burning his skin. "Milo!" she yells, looking around at his room. "What the hell are you both doing?"

I stare at the carpet.

"Just stuff," I say. "For my presentation."

Milo stares at the wall.

"Just stuff," he mumbles. "For Mima's presentation. I'm being Derek for her board."

Mum's zipping comes completely undone. She slumps down on Milo's bed and cradles her big pregnant belly egg in her arms.

"I just don't know what to do with the pair of you," she sobs, wringing her dress in her hands. "I'm trying my very best to keep things normal for you both. Trying to keep it all together... and..."

Guilt tugs at Milo's heart. He sits next to her and put his starfish hand on her arm.

"Sorry, Mummy," he says. "Don't cry."

She flusters her hands, waving them in front of her face to cool her temper down.

"I'm sorry, Milo," she says, kissing his head. "Mummy's OK. It's just..." And then another tearful tide sweeps her away. "It's just... look at this mess... and... everything and... your dad... and... the Bean due soon... and my hormones... and Granny... and... I don't know how much longer I can do this. God, I wish he'd just get a normal job! And Mima, your recent war obsession is driving me mad... and that horrible, horrible gas mask... I don't care if it's for school... for your presentation... it's just too creepy. If you hadn't noticed most of us on the camp are hoping the war will end and everyone will be home soon. We're just trying to get on like normal. It's not healthy to dwell on it. Why don't you get interested in something like puppies or dolphins or endangered species? Something cheerful like that?"

I pick up the gas mask and stroke its eyes. I'm sad she doesn't like it. There's nothing so terrible about it, is there? Dad would understand and it's only a stupid old mask, it's not the end of the world or anything. Mum looks at me with her big worried face and her voice cracks open.

"Oh, Mima!" she says. "What am I going to do with you?"

"You don't have to do anything with me, Mum," I say. "It's just a project. It's not that important; it doesn't mean anything, not really! Look, why don't you have a nice rest and I'll make you a cup of tea. Did you know that tea is Britain's national beverage? It's an interesting fact I learned when I was researching about the Blitz. Google says we wouldn't have won the war without it."

Mum drops her head in her hands and groans.

"Jemima," she says. "Please! Please! Please! Stop going on about war!"

Milo clings like a barnacle to her leg. "I made a good Derek, Mum," he says. "Mima said I was brilliant. I'm going to be in her film."

*   *   *

114

Later that night when I should be asleep I overhear Granny arguing with my mum. Their voices rise up the stairs like smoke.

"Well, I'm sorry, Bex," Granny says, "don't say I didn't warn you. You must have known what you were letting yourself in for when you married him. You only had to take a look at my life as an army wife to know."

"I don't know how you can say that," storms Mum. "I was in *love* with *your* son! I saw nothing but pink mist and fluffy bunnies and babies! All I really knew was that he was a soldier who took my breath away every time he put his damn uniform on and that he was a gentle giant who made my heart melt. I knew he'd be away a lot and that I'd have to learn to cope, but I didn't account for *this*!"

"I think you're making too much of the whole thing," says Granny. "She's only a child – you're blowing it out of all proportion, Bex."

"Blowing it out of proportion?" shrieks my mum. "I'm hardly overreacting! And this totally weird obsession of hers! I mean, did James spend his pocket money on gas masks as a child, like Jemima does? Did *he* dress his brother up as an evacuee? You don't have to live with her all the time. She's… she's… not normal. She's unnerving me. She doesn't even appear to have any proper friends and she's not interested in normal stuff that most twelve-year-old girls are interested in. She's moody and obsessive and quite frankly I don't know how to deal with her. And I blame it on the army. I blame it on James."

Granny sighs. I hear her stir her tea.

Then Mum whispers. "And do you know about her latest obsession? She keeps sitting in James's wardrobe! I mean, what in God's name is she doing that for? That's weirder than weird."

I creep along the landing to Mum's room and climb in Dad's wardrobe for a noseful of his smell and a stroke of his ghostly sleeve. I don't care if Mum thinks I'm weird. I like it in here. It makes me feel closer to Dad. What's weird about that? My fist raps the wood at the back of the wardrobe. Knocking to find the door to a magical world. Somewhere far away from my mum, with a lion called Aslan or a secret path to Afghanistan.

I stick my arms out of the wardrobe, open them wide and set a million angels free. They rise from my skin as inky blue shadows and flap through the gloom in a magnificent shimmer of light.

I wish I could climb on to one of their backs and fly over the trees, above the city, through the stars in search of the sun. I wish I could run away from my mum.

Chapter 11

She shows me the text...

Monday morning and part three of my Bring Dad Home mission is about to begin. First, I have a hot, hot shower and rub myself dry with the roughest towel in the airing cupboard so my whole body is shiny and pink. Then I stand in front of the mirror and pinch my cheeks until they flush. I can hear Mum and Milo in his room so I creep into her room, have a quick sniff of Dad's clothes and smudge some of her mascara under my eyes.

Hot red cheeks, check!

Tired grey eyes, check!

Starting to look ill, check!

Spots would be brilliant, but I don't know how to make them look real.

I groan my way downstairs.

"Graaannnyy," I moan. "I don't feel well. I need some hot tea."

"Tea's easy, pet," she says, pouring me a mugful. "It's still early though. Why don't you take your tea upstairs and snuggle in for a bit longer? I'll call you when it's time."

I nod and groan out of the kitchen and thump heavy tired feet up the stairs. Once I get to my room I drag my beanbag as close to the radiator as possible and sit down to sip my tea. I need to get burning feverish hot for part three of my plan to work.

When Granny calls, I thump back downstairs and flop on the kitchen sofa.

"I feel sooooo ill," I say. "I really think I need to stay at home. I can't go to school like this."

"What's the matter, pet?" she says, feeling my forehead.

"Arrgghh," I groan, pulling up my knees. "I don't know. I just feel so poorly, Granny. My head hurts and my tummy. I think I have something really bad."

Milo charges in making loads of noise. He zooms a blue toy plane in front of him and Mum follows on behind. She's holding her back with one hand and her heavy belly egg with the other. Her eyes are glassy and wide. I freeze and shift away from her. I don't understand how she could say such mean things about me. How could she think her own child is spooky and weird and unhinged? I wish I could stand on a chair and say to her, EXCUSE ME, BUT I'M NOT WEIRD OR SPOOKY OR UNHINGED. I'M JUST INTERESTED IN STUFF THAT YOU DON'T LIKE AND I'M MISSING MY DAD. JUST LIKE YOU ARE. I THINK YOU ARE MORE UNHINGED THAN ME!

But I don't. I droop my head low.

"Don't make so much noise, Milo," I groan. "My head hurts."

Mum looks at me. "What's the matter, Mima?" she says.

"I'm really, really poorly, Mummy," I say. "I think I need the doctor."

She puts her hand on my forehead, which by now has completely cooled down.

"You haven't got a fever," she says. "Show me your tongue."

I poke out my tongue while she inspects it. She's a detective looking for clues. She prods the glands in my neck. She pulls my eyelids wide open and takes a good deep look at my eyes. She makes me stretch out on my back while she presses my tummy.

"You seem fine to me," she says. "It's probably just wind. Pop off to school and if you get worse go to the sickroom and they'll call me."

Then she grips her belly egg and her eyes open wide again and her mouth makes a shape like an O. She bends over a little and groans. She clings on to the back of a chair to steady herself. She looks up at Granny who looks back at her.

A gush of water runs down her leg and puddles around her feet.

"Here goes!" she says. "The Bean is on its way!"

And as much as I'd like to cling on to my illness and stay at home to complete my plan, even I know that now is not the time to make a fuss.

"OooowwwW," says Mum. She grips the chair so hard her knuckles turn white. "I've been getting pains

121

on and off all night, but not as bad as these. Mima, call Georgie, quick, then get yourself dressed and on the bus." She throws her head back with pain. Granny pours some tea.

"OooowwwwW, James!" she cries into thin air. "Why aren't you here for us when we need you?"

I feel weird being at school knowing that the Bean is about to be born. At some point today I'm going to have a brother or a sister. I hope it's a sister. One boy is enough for any family and a sister would be much lovelier. We could be friends. I could take her out and show her all about the world.

The idea of the Bean being a sister sits like a little secret star, glowing in my tummy, keeping me warm. I wonder what we'll call her. Maybe Isobel, or Frejya, or Jane.

At lunchtime Jess bounces up to my table.

"You've got a brother!" she says. She pulls her phone out of her bag and shows me a text from her mum. "Look!"

Hi beautiful, Bex had baby boy. All easy. Tell Mima they'll be home when she gets back from school. Luv U xx

My warm glow turns to ice. I wish I could stand up on a chair and say, EXCUSE ME, JESS, BUT DON'T YOU THINK I MIGHT HAVE PREFERRED TO FIND OUT ABOUT MY OWN BABY BROTHER FROM MY OWN MUM OR MY OWN GRANNY? DON'T YOU REALISE YOU HAVE SPOILT A BIG SURPRISE. BABIES BEING BORN ARE FAMILY THINGS. NOT FOR NOSY PEOPLE LIKE YOU!

My appetite slides away. Jess rattles on.

"Me and Mum were only saying last night," she says, "how terrible it would be if something happened to your dad. He might never get to see his son. Imagine! And then the Bean would never get to meet his dad. It would be so tragic. Can you believe?"

Her eyes shine bright. My cauliflower cheese curdles with my juice.

I imagine my dad's head exploding on the sand, like in his films and then him in a coffin, in a big black car, like on the news.

Jess's eyes dull down.

"I wish my mum would have a baby," she says. "Being an only child is rubbish. It's too lonely." She looks at me. "Don't tell anyone, will you?" she says. "But it's scary when they shout, you know, my mum and dad. I hear them at night."

Ned plonks himself down, interrupting.

"I can't decide what to do my presentation on," he says. "Anyone got any good ideas?"

Tory Halligan and her parrots flutter up and peck away at their lunch. Tory slides in next to Ned and bats her eyelashes at him.

"I'm doing mine on fashion," she says. "How about I do mine on girls' fashion and you can do yours on boys? We could work on it together then, out of school time."

Ned rolls his eyes and looks up to the heavens.

"Girls," he sighs. "You're so predictable. I want to do something more interesting than fashion, but I can't think what."

"Jemima's got a new baby brother," says Jess. "Haven't you, Mima? Maybe you could do something on babies, Ned," she giggles. "Or teenage parents – that could be interesting. My mum was at the birth and Mima and I were just saying how terrible it would be if the Bean – that's what we call him – never got to meet his dad. You know, if his dad gets killed or something."

Ned brushes my face with his eyes and he's about to say something when Tory butts in.

"What are you doing yours on, Mima?" says Tory.

"Well," I say, "it's all about war and love and how war shreds hearts. My granny had this long-lost love…"

Tory and Jess and the parrots suddenly fall about laughing.

"Hi, Mrs Cassidy," giggles Tory in a silly voice. "My presentation is all about luuurrrvvve!"

Then they all join in, saying, "Luuurrrvvve! Luuurrrvvve! Luuurrrvvve!"

Laughter tears stream from their eyes.

I feel stupid now. My hearts blushes and closes in. My skin cringes and wants to fold up small and hide. I hate Tory Halligan. And Jess. And the rest of them and I'm never going to be able to do my presentation now. They'll split their sides laughing at me before I've even begun.

Ned's eyes land on me again and he mouths, "Just ignore them, Jemima Puddleduck."

The bus ride home is weird. I have a new brother. He is a whole entire brand-new human being in this world,

125

like no other human being ever before him. He's unique and he will sparkle with newness. We'll be connected through blood for the rest of our lives and I will watch him grow. Yet, when this most amazing thing was happening, I was at school, doing maths. This feels strange, like he has begun his life without me. It's a wonderful thing he finally hatched, but I'm sad he's not a sister and scared my heart won't stretch wide enough to wrap him in. I'm scared I might hate him for taking too much of everything. I'm scared my dad might love him more.

When I get back home, Mum's lying on the sofa in a jungle of blankets and flowers. Her eyes beam and her cheeks are flushed with so much love that she doesn't appear to notice the mess.

"Come see, Mima," she says, pulling back the corner of a cloud-soft blanket, exposing a tiny pink face and a load of dark curly hair. "Isn't he gorgeous?"

I squeeze between the sofa and the coffee table and crumple in a heap of school uniform on the floor. Compared to the delicate little bundle in Mum's arms I feel like a giant clumsy elephant. My arms and legs are too much in the way.

"Here," she says, shuffling round to make space on the sofa for me, "hop up. You can hold him. I think he's going to have your eyes."

I'm so nervous. I wish I could run away and shrivel up small into a cold hard nut of hate. I don't want to like the Bean. I want a sister. But when Mum rests my little marshmallow brother in my arms and his miniscule hand takes hold of my finger, my heart opens as wide as a butterfly's wings and soars. I nestle my face in his warmth. He smells so perfect and new. "I'm going to show you the world when you get bigger," I whisper. "There are so many wonderful things to see. And I'll bring Dad home soon. I promise. You're going to love him so much. He's truly amazing. And you don't know this yet, but our dad is the pancake king."

I turn to Mum.

"The Bean is perfect," I say, watching his tiny chest rise and fall with his breath, his eyelids flicker with sleep.

I could snuggle him for ever and never move from this most spectacular moment in my life.

Milo slides into the room and glares at the Bean. I beckon him over and hold him close with my spare arm.

"It's OK, Milo," I say. "We can stretch our hearts and love him too."

And my heart feels as soft as the fluffy white down on an angel's wing and as warm and glowing as the sun.

Then Mum says something and everything inside me crashes like cold metal cars.

"Oh," she says, "we managed to get a special message through to Daddy. To tell him about the Bean and then he called back. In fact, Milo had only just put the phone down when you came in. He's well, Mima," she smiles. "Everything's OK, he's safe! I'm so sorry you missed him, sweetheart, but he sent you love and lots of special big hugs and hopes to speak to you next time."

Jagged diamond tears well up in my eyes.

"I can't believe I missed him!"

"Never mind, pet," says Granny, bustling in with tea. "He'll call again next week. Why don't you go and do your prep and let Mum have a rest?"

I go upstairs and hide in Dad's wardrobe. His smell is fading. The air has changed to a musty tang. How come Milo got to speak to Dad and not me? And he would have just gone on and on about *Toy Story* and how much he loves Woody. He wouldn't have had a proper conversation. There's so much I need to talk about with Dad. It's so confusing being twelve! I think ten was better, or maybe even five. Or maybe the best time is newborn like the Bean because he has nothing to worry about, because the dust of bad things hasn't had a chance to settle on his skin. It's so confusing how one minute my heart was flying like a butterfly, full of love for our baby, and the next Mum's words flattened and squashed it into the ground.

I knock on the back of the wardrobe and wait to see if a secret path to a magical land will open up. I know it won't because I'm twelve now and I know about things like that, but if I were five, then maybe?

The lyrics to Kiss Twist's 'A Million Angels' spin through my mind and I pull up my shirtsleeves and set a million angels free. They lift from my arms like inky blue shadows. Soar through the sky like a radiant flash of white. Bravely swish and swoop and beat their wings towards the danger in the desert, towards the sun.

Chapter 12

I love you, Dad...

At last I get an e-bluey from Dad.

> Darling Mima,
>
> How are you?
>
> Sorry it's taken so long to write. It's been crazy
> here, but I'm safe and well and getting tired of the
> heat. The sun scorches down so hot you could fry
> an egg on the sand. Granny's never told me
> about this Derek. It must be her big secret. Sorry I
> can't be more helpful, but good luck trying to find
> him. I'm sure Granny will be pleased. Don't go
> getting into mischief though, will you? I need
> you to be good for Mummy. I can't wait to meet

the Bean; Mummy says he's just like you and me!

Being a baker or a potter wouldn't really work for me, precious. Granny's right – the army is in my bones. I can't help it.

In answer to your last question about killing people – my job is about protecting people, Mima, not hurting them, so that's what I try to do.

Good luck with your presentation, sweetheart. Remember to look out at your audience, speak up and focus, focus, focus.

Love you, pipsqueak xxx

I kiss my fingers, then touch his letter on my laptop screen.

I love you, Dad.

"Jemima Taylor-Jones," says Tory Halligan, breezing into the English room and plonking herself down on the seat next to mine. "I can't wait to hear all about luuurrrvvvve!"

She giggle-snorts until her eyes stream again with tears.

"You're so funny, Jemima!"

My face goes beetroot. I wish she'd just go away and sit in her usual place at the back. My heart is thumping hard enough at the thought of standing up in front of everyone and saying what I'm doing my presentation on without Tory Halligan making things worse.

The parrots flutter around. They flap and giggle and squawk, trying to find a place close to Tory.

"Go and sit somewhere else," Tory snaps at them. "You don't always have to follow me around. I want to sit next to Jemima for a change. I want to hear all about luuuurrrrvvvve."

Tory starts giggling again. Hayley, Sameena and Beth jump back like her words were a slap.

"You're so funny, Jemima," she laughs again. Then she leans in close and whispers in my ear, "Ned and Jemima sitting in the tree K.I.S.S.I.N.G." She moves even closer. "Except the thing is, Miss Taylor-Jones: hands off, OK? He's mine!"

Her words burn my ear and scorch my cheeks. I look like a boiled tomato I'm so red.

"You're welcome to him," I hiss. "I don't even fancy him."

"Well, let's keep it that way, shall we?"

Jess slides over and tries to knit herself in. "I'm doing my presentation on endangered species," she says. "'Cause did you know that loads of whales and dolphins are in danger because of shipping and fishing and oil? My mum says I can adopt one if I like and you get a poster and a registration card and everything."

Tory's eyes shoot Jess down in flames. "F.A.S.C.I.N.A.T.I.N.G, Jess. N.O.T!"

When Mrs Cassidy comes in, my head spins and my hands turn clammy with sweat.

First up at the front of the class is Tory. She strides up like she does presentations every day of the week, like they're as easy as cleaning her teeth. She's made loads of notes on little brightly coloured cards, to help her remember everything she wants to say. She speaks with the smile of a cat and a voice as clear as glass. Her presentation is going to be on fashion and her mum's taking her to a real fashion show as part of her research. She's going to customise loads of old clothes and do her own real live fashion show at school. She's going to charge an entrance fee and donate the money to a charity that gives special days out to sick children.

"Super work, Tory," chimes Mrs Cassidy. "I look forward to hearing the real thing."

Callum Richardson gets up totally unprepared and goes on and on for ages about football until Mrs Cassidy says she's heard enough and makes him sit back down. Then Hayley gets up and tells us that her presentation is going to be all about the history of chocolate. She's going to give us a live demonstration of how to make chocolate truffles and we'll all get a taste at the end.

The further round the class we go, the nearer it gets to being my turn. And the nearer it gets to being my turn the more the huge angel in my chest flaps to find a way out. My mouth is so dry my tongue keeps sticking to the inside of my cheek. I need a drink. I need a wee. I dry my sweaty hands on my skirt, but they go clammy again in seconds. My breakfast sloshes in my tummy. I think I might be sick.

I try to focus on Dad's lucky wish. I press it on my cheek on the spot where I hoped a flower would grow. *Focus, Jemima. Focus.* I take a deep breath like Dad told me to. I take a swig of water from my bottle. Nervous heat pushes through my skin.

When Jess gets up to tell us about her presentation on endangered dolphins and whales and the work of the World Wildlife Trust, Mrs Cassidy beams.

"Lovely idea, Jess," she smiles, smoothing a tail of hair behind her ear. "Maybe you could talk about endangered species in assembly and we could even see if the whole school could raise money for a dolphin?" Her eyes shine. "Perhaps everyone could find a way of raising money for charity? We've got Tory's children's charity and Jess's endangered species so far. I'm very proud of you all. Good work! I'm beginning to feel very inspired by all these super ideas!"

My stomach lurches like a rollercoaster.

Then Ned gets up and surprises us all.

"My presentation," he says, with a smile so wide it kisses my cheek like a butterfly, "is about John Lennon and peace. I'm a pacifist, which means I love peace and I hate war. I believe international disputes should be resolved peacefully, without fighting. That's what John Lennon was singing about and as part of my presentation I'm going to put together a Beatles tribute band. I need three other boys."

All the boys put their hands up. They jostle in their seats and shout, "Me! Me! Choose me, Ned!"

"Obviously," smiles Ned, "you need to be able to play an instrument and sing and obviously I'm going to be John Lennon on guitar."

When Ned's finished choosing his tribute band Mrs Cassidy turns to me.

"So, Jemima," she says. "Your turn."

My tummy flips. I want to do this, but I am soooooo scared. My shoes slap and squeak on the floor as I walk to the front of the class. They echo in the silence of everyone watching and waiting to hear me speak.

"My presentation," my voice cracks, "is all about the effects of war."

The whole class rise up with a Whhhhoooooa! Mrs Cassidy's eyes glitter with excitement.

"How wonderful," she says. "Maybe we can weave in a debate. On one side we'll have peace and on the other side we'll have war."

"Well," I continue, "it's not so much about war, it's really about love."

Tory Halligan and her parrots fall about laughing.

"It's about how war," I stutter, "shreds hearts. How it separates people who don't want to be separated. How it breaks up families."

I hold up the picture board of Granny and Derek.

"It all started when my granny gave me this box of old things. She started telling me about her life during the war and the Blitz and this childhood sweetheart she'd had. This long-lost love and…"

More whoops and hoots rise like steam from the back of the class. Tory almost falls off her chair she's snorting so hard with hysterics. She presses her hand over her mouth trying to brick them back in.

I try to focus like my dad said. I take a breath and look out at the class.

"… and I want to try and find him for her." I say. "I want to bring him back home to my granny. Before she dies. So she can stop wondering."

Out of the corner of my eye I see Ned give me a thumbs up.

"And," I say, "I want to bring home my dad too. For me and Milo and Mum and so he can meet our new baby, the Bean."

And then the room starts swimming in front of my eyes and the floor slips far away.

"Are you OK, Jemima?" asks Mrs Cassidy, looming her face so close I can see little flecks of mascara like

137

black snow that has settled on her cheek. I wish I could steady my hand enough to sweep them away because I know she'd be embarrassed for me to notice them. But I'm shaking too much. Then everything goes black and I fall down a dark, dark tunnel to the blackest, deepest bottom of the world.

"Stand back!"

Mrs Cassidy's voice breaks through the gloom.

"Give her some air," she says. "Somebody call the nurse."

"I think she fainted, miss," says Ned.

"Yes, Ned," she snaps, "I'm well aware of that."

In the sickroom Mrs Spencer brings me a glass of water.

"How are you feeling now?"

And I'm about to say, I'm feeling a bit better, thank you and I think I just fainted with nerves, when I realise that this is a perfect chance to relaunch part three of my Bring Dad Home mission.

"I feel terrible," I say. "Everything's all blurry and I feel sick. Maybe I need to go to the hospital? Maybe it's something really bad?"

But Mrs Spencer doesn't call the hospital. She calls my mum instead.

When Mum arrives, I feel really guilty. She looks so tired from nights awake with the Bean and she should probably still be cosy on the sofa, not here at school worrying about me. But I need to get Dad home. I can't miss out on this chance.

"Oooowwww," I say. I cover my eyes with my arm. "Now my head hurts. Oooowwwww, can you turn the lights off, please – they're too bright." I peer up at Mum. "I think it might be meningitis."

Mum and Mrs Spencer exchange a frightened glance. Mrs Spencer whips a thermometer from the cupboard and slips it under my arm.

"Oooowwww," I groan. "I think I'm going to be sick. Oooowwwww."

I try to remember the swirly feeling just before I fainted. I need my tummy to churn again. I need to make myself sick.

"Oooowwwww, please! Ooooowwww! I need an ambulance!"

Mrs Spencer slides the thermometer out.

"Her temperature's normal," she says. "I think it's just

139

a migraine that made her faint. Mrs Cassidy said the classroom was very warm. I'll give her some paracetamol for the pain. Take her home and let her sleep it off. She'll be right as rain by morning."

But Mrs Spencer is wrong. I won't be right as rain until my Bring Dad Home mission works, until my dad is back with us, where he belongs.

Chapter 13

I think my family have forgotten about me...

When we get back home, Mum makes me a nest on the sofa.

"Try and sleep it off," she says.

But I can't sleep. I have too much stuff whizzing around my head. I need to be much more ill than this for the army to send my dad back home.

I clutch my tummy.

"Ooooowww," I cry. "Mum, I think I might have appendicitis. I'm in so much pain. I really need the hospital or at least the doctor."

"You said it was meningitis an hour ago," she says. "Jemima, where exactly is the pain?"

"It's here," I say, pointing to my head. "And here." I clutch my tummy again and twist my body so it looks like I'm in pain.

She slides the thermometer under my arm and rests her hand on my forehead.

"You don't have a fever," she says, checking the thermometer reading, "and you'd definitely have one if it was meningitis *or* appendicitis. Mrs Spencer's right, it's probably just a migraine, Mima. Let's get you upstairs; we'll pull your blind down and make the room dark. Drink plenty of water and probably best to avoid food for a while."

So here I am. In the dark. Alone. With nothing to do.

I'm bored and I can't see anything. I pull my gas mask on and breathe. I need to make more noise, create more fuss then they'll have to take me to hospital. Mum wouldn't be being a good parent if she watched me be in so much pain for too long. I pull the gas mask off and stuff it under my bed.

"Muuuumm," I call. "Graannnyy, I feel so ill. Oooowww!"

Granny thuds up the stairs. She perches on the edge of my bed.

142

"What's really up, pet," she says, "because you don't look ill to me. You look the perfect picture of health. Are you worried about something? Someone upset you?"

"I fainted," I say. "I'd just shared my presentation idea and then everything went really dark, like I was falling into a big black hole. I'm not pretending, Granny – I really do think something terribly bad is wrong with me and I'm scared. I'm scared I might die."

She prods my tummy and tells me to lie on my side and raise up my knees.

"See, you wouldn't be able to do that, pet," she says, "if it were appendicitis – it would be too painful. I think you've got schoolitis more like or something else. A duvet day should put you right. Lots of rest. Like Mum says: no food for a bit. Have you emptied your bowels today, Mima? Might just be a bit of wind. Something disagreed. Mum's off to baby yoga after lunch, but I'll be downstairs if you need me."

I turn beetroot because of Granny asking about my bowels. Of course I've been today! And then she leaves me in the dark room again. Alone. I try sleeping, but I can't get comfy and I'm not even tired. I lie on my back and imagine I'm an angel soaring across the sky to my dad. I feel around my shoulder blades to see if any wings are sprouting. It would be so cool to have them hiding there under my top, then I could fly away whenever I please. I open my arms and set a million angels free. They hover in the blue shadows, then flash from my room like lightning. They fly through the camp sprinkling angel dust along their way. Flapping their great white wings towards my dad. I see him sleeping in the dark of the desert, in the cold night air, with a trillion bright stars sparkling in the sky. And they'll fly into his room and settle round his bed. Watching him. Guarding him. Keeping him safe.

I wish he'd call again. I need to hear his voice.

"Mmuuuuuuummm!" I call. "Don't forget to call me if Dad phones."

Then I remember that he won't be allowed to call again until next week.

I have to stay home. I have to stay home. I have to stay home.

I can hear everything going on downstairs but I'm a thousand miles away from them. I'm trapped on the island of my bed, in the bubble of my room.

The Bean cries out for a feed. Mum bustles around, getting ready for yoga. Granny clatters in the kitchen making lunch. My tummy grumbles and grinds like a peppermill when yummy soup smells float up the stairs. There must be something else I can do. If only I could somehow find a way of getting to hospital and staying there long enough for Dad to be called back home. It wouldn't be terrible. No one would get hurt and I'd get to have Dad back home and he'd get to meet the Bean. Everyone would thank me in the end. And even Dad said he's tired of the heat.

Maybe breaking a bone would work? That's a serious thing. I fling my arm against the wall. Ouch! I could probably make myself trip down the stairs. But then I might actually break my neck and die, and Dad would definitely come home then, but I wouldn't be here to see him. I need to think harder and better than this. I pull on my gas mask again and breathe and start thinking about Derek. I have to find him and bring him back to Granny otherwise my presentation will be rubbish. I'll have nothing to show. But how do you even start finding someone who has been lost for the past seventy-one years?

I turn over and lie on my tummy. It's all useless and rubbish. *I'm* useless and rubbish. I wish I could have the Bean here in bed with me – I want to talk to him about the world.

I'm here alone for hours and hours and hours. Mum comes back from yoga, Milo gets home from school and the TV is blaring through the ceiling. I'm just lying here trying to find a way to make my plan work.

I think my family have forgotten about me.

The doorbell rings. Granny is talking to someone. There's a thud, thud, thud up the stairs and a tap, tap, tap on my door.

I take a sharp breath in.

"Who's there?"

In my wildest dreams I imagine it's my dad come home. I don't know why, but maybe the angels worked, maybe they've really brought him home. Maybe the war has suddenly ended and he thought he'd give us a lovely surprise.

"Hey," says a voice, "it's me, Ned."

Then Ned appears in my room with a guitar slung over his shoulder.

"Ned! What are you doing in my house? In my room?"

I shuffle around and sit up. I smooth down my hair. At least I'm not wearing my pyjamas!

"Hey," he says, sitting on my bed. "I just wanted to make sure you're OK. I could hardly believe it – one minute you were up there talking about your presentation and the next you were splat down on the floor."

He strums a few chords on his guitar. The sound ripples through me like silk.

"How d'you even know where I live?"

"Jess," he smiles. "I came on my bike; it's not that far. Never been to an army camp before – it's weird."

"You get used to it," I say, "just like anything else."

I'm fluttering inside and I don't know why and I can't stop twiddling my hair.

"Are you still ill?" he asks.

"I never really was," I whisper. "I think I just fainted through nerves. I hate speaking in public. It's so embarrassing. But I really want to do this presentation. I really want to help my granny."

"It was a pretty impressive slide to the floor," he smiles, getting up and opening my blind. "Like something out of a film."

The sunlight kisses his halo hair and if Ned were to

grow wings he would make an awesome angel. I've never had a boy sit on my bed before, except Milo. In fact I've never even had a boy visit me at home. In fact, in fact, I've never even had a boy talk to me. Not *really* talk to me, because he wanted to. I've never known anyone like Ned.

"Can I tell you a secret?" I whisper. "I'm going to burst if I don't tell someone."

Ned pulls his skinny-jeaned legs up on the bed, crosses them and turns to face me. He strums his guitar and sings the verse of the John Lennon song about peace. His green Converse laces trail across my bed like vines.

"I'm all ears for you, Jemima Puddleduck," he smiles.

"Well," I whisper, "I have this plan to get my dad back home and I'm trying to make something bad enough happen so that the army will *have* to put him on a plane. I don't like him being in the army. I want him here with me, doing a normal job. You might be campaigning for peace, Ned, but I'm standing up for love and no matter what I fight for I will rearrange the alphabet and put U and I next to each other and then you'll finally notice."

I blush.

"I mean, I'll rearrange the alphabet and put my dad next to me and then he'll finally notice that I need him here, not across the other side of the planet. I will do it, Ned. I have to. It's not fair. Thousands of families get split up every year because of stupid wars. Millions of hearts get broken."

Ned sighs. "Jemima Puddleduck," he says, resting his finger on my foot, "you can't play God and go around rearranging the alphabet for anyone. Families get split up for all sorts of reasons, every day; it's not just war that does it. Enough bad things happen in this world without you making more."

"Well, what am I supposed to do then?" I snap. "Just wait around and do nothing? Wait until we get a phone call saying he's dead?"

"You just have to trust," he says. "I know I don't believe in war and I said your dad's stupid for putting his life at risk, but he must have his reasons, Jemima Puddleduck, and maybe you should respect them and let him get on with his job."

"It's all right for you," I snap. "You have a cosy little life. You don't know what it's like."

I huff down in my bed and cover my head with my pillow.

"Leave me alone, Ned." I snap. "I wish I'd never told you. You don't know anything!"

"Suit yourself," he says, heading towards the door, "but for your information, apart from checking out how you were after your fainting fit, I also came to say I've been talking to my gramps about that Derek bloke. He might be able to help. But... whatever!"

He opens the door. I peep out from under my pillow and I hear him mutter under his breath, "You know nothing about my life either, Jemima Puddleduck, because I promise you, it's not all roses."

He shuts the door, then seconds later peeps his head back round.

"So it *was* you that set off the fire alarms. I knew it! You've been acting so weird lately, Jemima. If you thought no one noticed you keep sliding off on your own at lunchtimes, you thought wrong, because I did. How could you be so dumb, Jemima? I've fooled myself. I thought you were made of better stuff than that!"

The door clicks shut.

I am made of better stuff, Ned, if you really want to

know. And that's exactly why I'm doing what I'm doing. Without my Bring Dad Home mission he stands no chance of getting home.

At least I'm trying to help!

Chapter 14

I'm not going, I snap...

I've given up pretending to be ill. It's boring. It's boring, boring, boring lying up here alone listening to all the interesting things going on downstairs. Granny's really busy in the kitchen. She's creating loads of yummy things to eat and the delicious cooking smells keep wafting up the stairs to tempt me. Then every time I tell her I'm hungry she says the food she is making is not for me! I can't believe my own granny is being so mean. She says I can have tasty things when I'm better, but for now I'm only allowed dry toast or boring vegetable broth or disgusting lemon and honey tea! I think I need to make myself better very soon. Before I starve to death.

I need to put some serious thought into my Bring Dad Home mission. I need to make something much bigger happen, something much more serious. And I don't care about Ned. What does he know about anything anyway? He should try being me for a day because apparently I'm unhinged!

It's Saturday and we're sitting around trying to choose a name for the Bean.

"I think Derek's a grand name for a boy," says Granny. "You can't go wrong with a name like that."

Mum laughs and rolls her eyes.

"I think we should call him Woody," says Milo. "Woody's a cool name."

"Whatever it is," says Mum, "it needs to work on a birthday card. You know, *Lots of love from James, Bex, Jemima, Milo and…*"

A worrying thought sits on my tongue, but I'm too scared to speak it.

If my dad dies before we register the Bean's name I know we'll call him James.

"How about James?" I say. "After Dad."

"Not James," says Mum. "Too confusing."

Then the phone goes.

We all take a sharp breath in and stretch our ears. We all hope it's Dad, calling to say hello.

"Hi," says Mum.

I stretch my ears as far as I can down the phone, listening out for his voice.

"Yes, I'm sure she'd love to! Thanks, Georgie! You're a star! Yes, twenty minutes. She'll be ready."

"It was Georgie," says Mum, taking the Bean from Granny. "She's taking a gang of kids to the cinema and phoned to invite you, Mima. Isn't that lovely? They're picking you up on the way."

"I'm not going," I snap.

"Why ever not?" says Mum. "You'll have great fun."

"I just don't want to go," I snap. "No reason."

"You're going, Mima," she spits. "And that's that! You need to stop isolating yourself from everyone and start going out."

"I'm not going," I shout, running upstairs. "You can't make me, you don't understand."

I run upstairs and hide in Dad's wardrobe. I take a sniff of his fading smell. Then Granny comes up and opens the wardrobe door.

"Give it a try, pet," she smiles. "It mightn't be so bad as you'd imagine. You might even have a bit of fun."

"I won't, Granny," I plead, "I promise you. Please talk to Mum, please don't make me go! They keep laughing at me about my presentation."

Granny takes hold of one of Dad's sleeves and strokes it. She lifts it to her nose and smells.

"Come on, pet," she soothes. "Mum does have a point; it's not healthy for a girl your age to be home all the time."

So here I am, *forced* to wait on the drive for Georgie's car. I kick the gravel. I didn't even get to suggest a proper name for the Bean – I only thought of Dad's. My stomach is in overdrive, churning my lunch around, making me sick.

Pip. *We're on our way! My dad just called. Did yours? He had a lucky escape today. A bomb nearly went off in his face.*

I flick an angel off my arm. Please be safe, Dad. Please be safe! Please be safe!

I listen for the phone. I can't go now. He might call. If only my mum would understand how I feel. But she never understands me. That's Dad's job. Not hers! I don't see any problem with staying at home anyway. I'll go out when I'm ready. I'm a person, I have *rights*; she can't *make* me go!

I open the front door and peep my head inside.

"I'm not going, Mum," I say. "Jess had a call from her dad, which means Dad might call us too, and I don't want to miss him again. And you can't make me go. I don't even feel well. I've got a headache. I think I'm going to be sick."

"Come on, sweetheart," says Mum, "it'll be good for you to get out, Mima, and Dad won't call, I promise. It's natural that you're a bit nervous. But you'll soon get over it. Next thing you know there'll be discos and boyfriends and all sorts of things."

She chuckles and lifts her eyebrows. My cheeks burn. My mum is gross. She is so old!

When Georgie swishes into the driveway her car tyres send gravel spitting and popping like corn. My knees tremble. I don't want to go. Jess is in the front and squashed in the back like sardines are Tory Halligan, Sameena and Beth. Georgie makes me squeeze in next to Tory, so close I can smell the fruity shampoo on her hair.

"Yay! What fun!" says Tory, smiling at me. "I can't think of a more fun day out."

I ignore Mum's wave as Georgie drives us away.

"Can we have a chat about fashion, Jemima," says Tory, "for my presentation? Oooh, I've an idea." Her eyes light up. "Can we have a sleepover afterwards, Georgie? Pleeeaasee? Then we can all get cosy and share more of our presentation ideas. It'll be fun. And Jemima, I want to hear more about luuuuurrrrrvvveeee."

Then everyone starts laughing. I hate them all.

"Yay!" says Jess. "Pleeeaaasssssseeee, Mum, please say yes to a sleepover!"

The cinema is full of kids jostling in the queue. Boys wearing skinny jeans and check shirts and gelled hair scuffle and play fight. Girls who stink of bubblegum flutter their lashes like bats. I touch the big bow on my head. I lace up my boots. I can't breathe. I need air. I think I'm going to faint. Inside I'm flapping about like a wet fish. Dying a slow and painful death on the slippery deck of a boat. I don't even *want* to look like these girls. I like what I wear. I don't *want* to fit in!

And Georgie isn't even staying with us for the film.

"You have fun," she chirrups, stuffing a big stash of cash in Jess's hands, "and I'll meet you all later in Pizza Express."

Now I have nothing to hold on to except popcorn and Coke and I'm scared of sliding down on to the floor.

"It's SO lovely having the vintage queen with us," says Tory. She turns to me. "Now, Jemima, tell me all about this army tie you're wearing? Is it one of your dad's?"

Then she spots something in the distance. She squeals and bobs around. Sameena and Beth watch her every move. They copy whatever she does. They jiggle and giggle. They squeal and bob. They choose the same sweets and the same drinks.

Jess stands in the shadows and hands out the cash.

"Neddy! Neddy!" Tory squeals, pushing through the crowd. "What a surprise to see you here!"

Ned comes to join us, with Callum Richardson jostling at his side.

"What are you going to see, Neddy?" says Tory, sliding her body against his. "The new *Pirates* or *Kung Fu Panda 2*?"

"Wouldn't miss Johnny Depp for a panda, would I?" says Ned, smiling. Then he turns and whispers to me, "Done any more dumb things today, Jemima Puddleduck, or have you learned to grow up?"

Chapter 15

Georgie's smile is as big as the sun...

It's better in the cinema. I like the dark because nobody can see how much I'm trembling. I hang on at the end of the line so I can sit near the aisle, in case I need to escape. Tory drags Ned in next to her. Another bird in her nest. The rest follow with Jess at the end and then me. My brain is a bee buzzing from topic to topic, trying to find something fun and interesting to say. But every time I land on something I think might work, someone else makes a better joke or comment and swats mine away. I don't even know why I feel so jumpy. I'm sitting next to Jess and I've known her for a hundred years. But it's different being out together, all alone, without our mums. I wish my mum would understand things like that and let me be alone in peace.

Eventually I find some words.

"How's your dolphin collection going, Jess?"

Her eyes squash me flat and twist me under her shoe.

"How's your pathetic gas mask one and those stupid angels?"

When the titles roll and Johnny Depp's pirate face flashes across the screen, I whisper into her ear, "Why did you even invite me, Jess?"

"I didn't invite you," she snaps, piercing my skin with her stare. "My mum did. I've got new friends now, real friends, and I don't need to hang out with you. But your mum's so worried about you because she thinks you're a freak, so she asked my mum if we could invite you along. Then my mum goes off shopping and I get dumped with you! Brilliant! Let's face it, Jemima, we've only hung out together because we've had to, because of the stupid army. I never really liked you, you know."

My cheeks burn as great waves of cinema sound crash over my head.

"And I've never really liked you either, Jess," I say,

"so that makes two of us. And I don't want to be here any more than you want me to be."

I wish I could stand up on the cinema chair and say to Jess, AND IF YOU REALLY WANT TO KNOW, I'D RATHER BE AT HOME WAITING TO SEE IF MY DAD MIGHT CALL. But I don't. I slide down in my seat and slurp on my Coke. I really need to talk to Dad; I just need to hear his voice, then I'll feel better for a while. I can't believe my mum *asked* Georgie if she would invite me to the cinema. It's so embarrassing! Why does she always have to stick her big nose in?

About halfway through the film Ned squeezes past me for the loo and five minutes later he's back.

"I don't understand you," he whispers. "I thought you were nice. I thought you were different to the rest."

Now the film is a blur and I don't even know why I'm crying. Twelve is so confusing! My eyes keep pulling themselves over to ogle at Ned and Tory. They're all cosy in close together. Sharing their popcorn.

I don't know what's wrong with me. I don't even *like* Ned.

After the cinema Tory Halligan begs Ned to come with us to Pizza Express.

162

"Please come, Neddy," she squawks. "It'll be fun."

She looks at Jess. "Your mum wouldn't mind paying for Neddy and Callum too, would she, Jess?"

"No, she won't mind," says Jess.

"Yay! Please come, Neddy."

"I'll have to call home first," says Ned, "just to let my gramps know where I am."

Tory rolls her eyes in her head. "That is *so* childish, Neddy," she says.

Ned's eyes blaze. "Well in case you haven't noticed," he says, pulling out his phone, "we are still children. And anyway this call has nothing to do with being *childish*, Tory, it's more to do with caring about other people." He laughs, then bumps his shoulder against hers in a jokey way. "So shallow, Tory Halligan. Only interested in yourself!"

Beth mouths K.I.S.S.I.N.G. and her and Sameena fall about sniggering. A jealous dagger twists in my heart and I don't even know why.

Jess pushes closer to Ned, trying to be part of the fun, but he rolls his eyes at them all and pulls out his phone.

"It's OK, Gramps," I hear him say, "I won't be too

163

late, I promise… That's right, you have another cup of tea and I'll be back before you know it."

I wish I didn't have to go to Pizza Express. I wish I could just go home. Ned won't speak to me, I don't want to speak to Jess and I'm scared of Tory's tongue.

I sit as far away from Tory Halligan as possible. I can't trust her words, they're too confusing. Her nicey nicey voice makes her *sound* like she really might want to get friendly with me and talk about my clothes for her presentation, but there's something in her eyes I don't trust.

Georgie sits alone at a table in the corner. She reads a magazine. She sips coffee while we choose our food.

"I'll leave you kids to it," she giggles from her table. "You don't want an old fogey like me messing up your fun. Order what you like. The bill's on me."

"Yay! You're so *kind*, Georgie," smirks Tory Halligan. "So *generous*. I wish you were my mum."

"Yay!" says Jess, beaming like a torch on a dark night. "Then we would be sisters, Tory. I've always wanted a sister. That would be the best!"

Georgie's smile is as big as the sun.

I wish I were as good as Tory at sewing and weaving

people in. She draws them close to her with her big shiny smile, then sets to work stitching them on. And there they stay like colourful little patches on a beautiful handmade quilt. I'm more like a boat. Every time I bob a little bit close to someone a huge tide comes and sails them away. Just like Ned really, and I thought he liked me. He came to my house with his guitar and everything.

I can't eat much. The pizza crust sticks in my throat. My mind buzzes around for something interesting to say. Ned and Callum make jokes and do tricks. The parrots split their sides with laughter that tinkles through the air. Georgie's smile stretches over to our table. Her big pink-lipped mouth tells us to order more food.

When we're piling through the door to leave, Ned turns to Tory to say goodbye.

"Thanks for suggesting I come along," he says. "It's been more fun hanging out with you than I expected."

I watch the evening sun kiss his halo of curls and the jealous dagger stabs me again. I keep telling myself, *I'm not jealous! I'm not jealous! I'm not jealous!*

Chapter 16

Her eyes glow...

Back in the car Tory Halligan smells of mozzarella cheese and she sounds like a scary clockwork doll gone mad. Her eyes swivel in her head and words bubble out of her mouth like champagne.

"Can we have a sleepover, Georgie? Can we?" she bubbles. "Pleeeaasssse, pleeeaasssse. You're so lovely, Georgie; I wish my mum were as kind as you. And I've never been to an army camp before. It would be such fun!"

"Can we, Mum? Pleeeaasssee?" parrots Jess. "You're the best mum in the world, I promise."

"OK!" squeals Georgie. "Why not? Call your

mums and we'll have a drive around to collect your stuff."

"Sorry, I don't think I can make it," I say. "I have some prep to do."

"Prep! Prep! Prep!" says Tory. "You're crazy about prep, Jemima. Let your hair down just this once and come out and have some fun." Her eyes swivel again and stab me with blue. "I promise you, Jemima, we're going to have *such* fun! The problem with you is that you're so serious about everything. You've never learned to have fun." She's quiet for a moment. Her mind concentrates hard. "Do you know what, Jemima?" she squeals at last. "I'm going to make it my personal job to teach you all about fun before it's too late." A high-pitched laugh ripples from her throat. "And you can teach me all about fashion in return! Laugh out loud!"

I wish I could stand up on top of Georgie's car and shout, I DO NOT WANT TO COME TO YOUR STUPID SLEEPOVER. I DO NOT LIKE YOUR IDEA OF FUN. But I don't. Instead, I say, "No, really, I need to do some work on my presentation."

Jess turns her sly eyes on me. "If Jemima thinks her

work is more important than having fun, then maybe she *should* go home." She looks at Tory. "We can still have fun on our own."

"But I want Jemima!" sulks Tory. "I want all of us! Shame Neddy couldn't come too."

Then Georgie chips in. "Oh, sweetie," she says, looking at me. "You come too. Like Tory says, it'll be fun."

"No," I say. "I really do need to get on with my presentation. I'm behind with it already. There's so much stuff I still have to do."

But when I get home my mother has other ideas.

"You just need to push through this bit, Jemima," she says, packing my toothbrush and pyjamas into a bag, "and be brave. It's a great opportunity to make some friends and I'm not going to let you miss it. You're twelve years old and it's time you got out of the house. I promise you you're going to have a great time and then by next Saturday you'll be begging to have them all back for a sleepover here. And they all seem such lovely girls. All so pretty!"

"They're not lovely," I say. "I hate them, Mum. Especially Jess. There's nothing *fun* about being with them. Dad wouldn't make me. I refuse to go!"

"Oh, sweetheart," says Mum. "I'm sure you don't hate them, not really. You're just nervous. It's your first proper sleepover." She pulls me close, wraps me in her arms and strokes my cheek. "Come on, poppet. For me?"

Mothers are strong and their words can make you do stuff you don't want to do. I sigh and pull away from her. I stuff my sleepover things in a bag and drag myself back to the car.

After nearly three hours of being at Jess's, everyone's tired and wired with chocolate and fizzy drinks and cupcakes, and the strong smell of nail varnish is invading my nose. I'm tucked in my sleeping bag, in the corner of the room. I'm inking angels up and down my arms.

"What are *they*?" says Tory Halligan, sliding over and inspecting my arms. "God, Jemima, your arms look a mess!"

"They're angels," sniggers Jess. "Yay! Freaky Jemima blows them to her dad every day. She thinks they'll keep him safe. She went crazy drawing them on *everyone* the day our dads left. Her mum went completely mad! I mean, like my mum said, you can't go promising little kids that their mums and dads won't get killed in the war when it really isn't true. Can you? And they might, you know!"

Her eyes glow. She looks from girl to girl. Drawing them in.

"It's all right for you lot," she says, "but our dads actually might die! *We* might be on telly!"

The lump in my throat grows the size of a football and I keep repeating in my head, *Don't let him die! Don't let him die!*

"You're so funny! Jemima! So sweet!" Tory shrieks. "But Jess is right. Your dad'll need a bit more than biro angels to keep him alive. Haven't you seen the news lately? He's in big, big trouble over there. The Taliban have gone crazy and nobody knows if their friend is actually a friend any more or if they've turned into the enemy. And then my dad says that people like that will go on using taxpayers' money for years to come. The British Army needs to learn to stand up to the Americans, and say no to war, that's what my dad says."

She casts her eyes around the room and her words throw sharp arrows in my side.

They're both right about my angels. I know they are. I'm a stupid baby and my dad probably *will* die. I don't even know what Tory means about the taxpayers, but I do know that when I'm near her my body turns to milk. I have no bones left to hold me up and keep me strong. What I don't understand is what have I ever done to Tory to make her be this mean to me? It's not fair. It's the same with Jess. I know she says stuff about our dads getting hurt on purpose to upset me, and I wish it didn't, but it does. *She* does. And what's worse is when she pretends to be friendly. Everything is so confusing. Twelve is confusing, the most confusing time in my life.

Everyone starts playing hairdressers and beauticians with Georgie's hair straighteners and make-up. I slide down in my sleeping bag and blow a million angels to my dad. Tory and Jess might be right. I might be stupid and babyish. But I promised. I can't stop now. I blow them one by one, brilliant flapping flashes of radiant white. Zooming. Fluttering through the sparkling stars. Skirting around the shining moon. Heading towards the stifling desert, towards the baking sun.

To my dad.

To my own dad.

I wish he'd call home. I wish this war would end. I

wish someone, somewhere in the night would send a beautiful angel to me.

Tory Halligan is whipping up the room like egg whites. She's laughing hysterically from too much sugar but the devil is dancing in her eyes.

"I know!" she squeals. "Let's play a game." She gathers her flock round her on the bed. It's Jess's bed, but Jess is sleeping on the floor tonight because Tory Halligan is the queen.

"Yay! A game!" smiles Jess, her eyes sparkling in fairy-light glow. "How about Monopoly or Cluedo?"

Tory rolls her eyes. She sighs. "God, no! They're boring games, Jess. We need something a… a little more spicy than that. We mustn't forget we need to teach Jemima about fun! Real fun!"

Her eyes glitter over to me. She's thinking. Thinking. I'm shrinking. Shrinking.

"I know," she says, squealing like a pig, "how about Truth or Dare? What do you think, Jemima, Truth or Dare?"

I hate Truth or Dare. I look in her eyes and can tell that something evil is stewing in her brain.

"You play," I say, sliding further into my sleeping bag. "I'm too sleepy."

"No, no, no," says Tory, fluttering Sameena, Jess and Beth away. She pats the warm patch on the bed next to her. "I *want* you to join in, Jemima, this is part of your education on fun, and anyway the game wouldn't be the same without *you*. Freaky girls always have such *interesting* things to tell."

I wish I could stand up and say, GO TO HELL, TORY HALLIGAN AND THE REST OF YOU. I WILL NOT PLAY YOUR GAME.

But true life isn't my imagination, true life is real, and I watch myself slide out of my slippery nest and slither towards the queen.

"Now, who's turn is it first?" she says, swivelling her eyes around the room. Sameena, Beth and Jess shrink back; even they can see the poison on her tongue.

I freeze like a dummy on the bed.

"I know…" She smiles, turning her gaze on me. "How about…?"

Tory is thinking hard. Her eyes press into me and bruise my skin.

"How about…?" She slowly pokes out her tongue and pops her pink chewing gum. "I know!" she squeals. "Let's take a vote."

"Yay!" says Jess. "Let's take a vote."

Tory's eyes land on Jess. "Shut up, Jess!" she snaps. "Stop copying me! You're getting on my nerves. You're boring. Can't you think of your own thing to say for once?"

Tory's words bite Jess. She shrinks into her skin and her beady eyes sparkle like black gems.

"No!" says Jess. "Let's not take a vote. It's my sleepover and I say Jemima's first." She looks at me. "Truth or Dare?"

I'm dead. I wish I *were* dead. I hate Truth because they'll laugh at anything I say so I swallow hard and go for Dare.

"Yay!" says Jess, "I LOVE dares. OK, I dare you, Jemima, to eat a whole tub of ice cream in one go."

"No! That's a lame dare," says Tory. "How about…"

"How about make a phone call to a random number and make kissing noises down the phone?" says Beth.

"Mmmm, less lame," says Tory, "but it's still not it."

My heart thumps. Please someone send me an angel.

"OOOH, I've got it," says Tory Halligan, grabbing my arm and jiggling up and down. "I dare you to take off all your clothes and have a freezing cold shower for one whole minute."

174

I look from Tory to Jess to Sameena to Beth, hoping someone might rescue me. All their eyes are blank and closed.

I take a deep breath.

"OK," I brave, "I'll do it!"

I head for the bathroom and am about to close the door when Tory Halligan puts her foot in the way.

"No, no, no!" she cackles. "You have to do it in public, Jemima. Otherwise we won't know if you really got in."

She runs the shower until it's *freezing* cold, then steps back and invites me in. It's not the cold water I'm worried about. Cold water's not so bad. It's taking my clothes off in front of everyone. That's what I hate. It's different at school, after games, because everyone gets in. But they're all watching me now. Like I'm on TV. They're all looking with wide eyes. Zipping their giggles inside.

My fingers tremble on my buttons and slip and slide on my clothes. I'm having second thoughts.

"What if I don't do it?" I ask.

Tory's laughter cuts the air. "You'll have to do a forfeit," she smirks. "Which, believe me, will be way worse than this, and it will definitely include snogging a B.O.Y!"

Chapter 17

OH! MY! GOD!

The shower is not terrible. It does freeze all the nerve endings under my skin and make me jangle with pain, but I manage to turn my back on everyone so they can't really see. If I don't make a fuss hopefully they'll leave me alone. I even manage to say, "Yay! You're a good teacher, Tory. This is actually quite good fun." I flick a few drops of icy water out to them and make a fake laugh. They squeal! Squealing is good. Maybe this is how you make friends. Maybe this is what messing about is like. Maybe this is what they want! I take a deep breath and cup my hands, then I fill the cup with freezing water and throw it out of the shower.

Tory Halligan shrieks!

"You've soaked me!" she screeches. "Look at what you've done!" She grabs a towel. "Look at me! I'm soaked through!"

"I didn't mean to soak you," I say. "I was just having fun."

"I am so getting you back for this, Jemima Taylor-Jones." Her eyes scald my skin. "*Nobody* does that kind of thing to *me!*"

I turn the shower off and lean out for a towel. My hand grabs the corner of one, but Tory snaps it away. She clucks and clucks like mad and starts grabbing armfuls of towels.

"Let's throw them out the window," she shrieks. "All of them! That'll get you back."

She opens the window and bundles them into the night.

Jess squeals like a fat pig. She grabs my clothes from the floor and stuffs them into Tory's hands. Tory turns back to the window. I shiver. Beth and Sameena stand on the edge with wide glass eyes.

"You can't do that!" I shriek. "It's not fair. I've done my dare, now it's someone else's turn."

177

"I can do what I like," snaps Tory. "I always do!"

Jess runs to the bedroom for the rest of my stuff. I'm freezing to death. I try to cover myself up with my hands and pull my stuff from Tory at the same time.

"Stop it!" I scream. "Give me back my clothes."

Sameena and Beth squeal. They're in a frenzy now and Tory is up on the window ledge. She hangs out of the window, flapping my clothes like flags. I edge in next to her. My damp cold skin slips on the tiles and the chill night air whispers over my skin.

I reach for my top. It's in her hand. Shining angel white under the moon. Flapping wildly in the wind. I don't like the wind.

"Sorry, freak," taunts Tory Halligan. "You can't have them back unless you go out and get them. Ha! Ha! Ha!"

And one by one she drops my things.

"Give them back, Tory," I shout. "This isn't fun. You can't do this."

"Watch me!" she says, leaning further and further away.

Jess brings my sleeping bag and pyjamas and rucksack in. She passes them to Tory. I'm piggy-in-the-middle and I reach and stretch to grab something, *anything* to cover me up.

"Please!" I say. Tears prick the back of my eyes. I stand up on the window ledge and shout, "DON'T DO THIS TO ME! PLEASE!"

They all freeze for a moment, then Tory's eyes flame like wildfire. She dangles my knickers in front of my eyes and laughs.

"Want them?" she squawks.

Sameena and Beth giggle. Jess has gone mad. She's ready to throw the contents of the entire house outside.

I grab for my knickers. Tory flicks them away. Armies of goosebumps march on my skin. I climb off the window ledge.

"Just give them to me," I scream, flying at her. She jerks backwards, waving them out in the wind. Showing them off to the stars.

"Stinky knickers!" she taunts. "Stinky knickers! Stinky knickers! Stinky knickers!"

Then the others join in. I'm drowning in sound.

"Stinky knickers! Stinky knickers! Stinky knickers!"

"Give them here," I shriek. I climb back on the window ledge and stretch my arm out towards her hand.

179

"Stinky knickers! Stinky knickers!"

I reach further and further out. Tory Halligan stretches further and further away.

"I *hate* you, Tory Halligan," I scream. "I wish you were *dead*!" My words slice the air like a kite string. "Give them back to me! Please!"

And then she stretches just one millimetre too far and for a moment I think we're both going to fall. Then an idea rips through my brain like lightning. A smooth sense of calm settles like snow on my skin.

At last! I've found a way.

This is it!

The *final* most *perfect* piece of my Bring Dad Home mission.

I glance at the others, then at Tory. I can do this. I have to.

I have no choice.

Dark moon shadows loom on the lawn below. A gnarled black-silhouetted tree cracks and creaks in the wind.

Imagine you're an angel, I say to myself. *Come on! You can do it! Come on, Jemima…*

Fly!

This is the bad-enough thing I've been looking for. This will *definitely* bring my dad back home.

I stretch my arms out wide and imagine a million soft feathers fluttering on my wings. My skin is alabaster white. I'm dazzling under the stars.

And I'm about to fly towards the silvery moon when Tory grabs hold of my leg.

"GET OFF!" I shriek, pushing her away. "LEAVE ME ALONE!"

She grips me tighter.

"Stop it!" says Tory. "You're mad!"

I grip her shoulders to push her away.

"Come down from the window," screeches Sameena. "Both of you! You're scaring me."

The wind catches the window and rips it wide open with a howl. Shampoo and conditioner bottles clatter and skid like skittles on the tiles. We wobble and topple. I try to push Tory back indoors. I edge myself out. She pulls me back.

"What are you doing?" I scream. "Leave me alone!"

My foot slips on the tiles. I crash into Tory. She clings on to me. I need to shake her off.

I have to close my eyes...

I have to fly.

The wind whirls and whips my skin and a huge gust swallows us whole. We topple. We catch each other's gaze. Terror blazes in our eyes as I slip off the window ledge and thud on the tiles and Tory Halligan tumbles through the night and into the garden below.

A deafening silence fills the room.

Then Jess screams.

Her shrill voice drills the air and bounces off the walls. We scrabble to the window. We peer out and look down at Tory Halligan's body. She's lying crooked and deathly still on the ground.

We're white as statues, as pale as the moon. I'm freezing. Icy cold.

Georgie bump, bump, bumps up the stairs.

"What on earth's going on?" she shouts, coming into the bathroom. Her eyes flicker around the room looking for clues. When they land on the open window, she pushes us out of the way, leans forward and gasps.

"OH! MY! GOD!" She screams.

She peers down into the garden. Horror sweeps up her face. Then suddenly everyone clucks and screeches and scrambles downstairs. I'm left in the bathroom alone. Icy tears stream from my eyes. My teeth chatter. I'm so cold I might die from hypothermia. I run into Jess's room, wrap myself in her duvet and rush downstairs.

Under the stars Tory Halligan is lying perfectly still. Her face is as white as the moon. Her blonde hair is splayed out around her head, shining like a halo. Her leg is jutting out sideways, like it doesn't belong to her body any more.

"Stay back!" screams Georgie, throwing her arms out wide. "We mustn't move her. Jess, call an ambulance! Quick!"

Jess leaps into the house and makes the call.

My clothes and sleepover stuff are sprawled around the garden. Hanging from bushes. Dripping from the trees. Georgie cups her face in her hands. She rubs her eyes and scrapes her hands through her hair.

"OH! MY! GOD!" she says again. "What on earth happened?"

She turns to me.

"Give me the duvet, Jemima," she says, grabbing it. "We need to keep her warm. OH! MY! GOD! I'm going to have to call her mum. OH, MY, G—! Jemima, why are you naked?"

Her eyes spin around the garden photographing my clothes.

I stare at her. I'm speechless and my whole body is juddering with cold.

"I asked you a question, Jemima," she says. "Can you answer me, please?" She crouches down next to Tory Halligan. She strokes her face. She prods her neck for a pulse.

I scrabble around trying to gather my stuff, I grab my knickers from a bush and slip them on.

"What on earth was going on, girls?" shrieks Georgie. "I need to know. I thought you were having a disco or something. I thought the racket was you having fun. Not this!"

"We were playing Truth or Dare," I say, sliding my top over my head. "I was in the shower and everyone took my clothes…"

Jess joins us in the garden and whispers into the night. "The ambulance is on its way," she says. She stares at Tory. "Is she dead?"

"GET BACK!" screams Georgie, flapping her arms

wildly like the possibility of true death in her garden has only just occurred to her. "Get back indoors and stay away!"

I stare at Tory. That could be me. That *should* be me. *I* was the one who wanted to fall. Not Tory. Now I'll *never* get my dad back home.

We tumble indoors and wait in silence. The clock on the wall tick, tick, ticks. When the paramedics arrive we follow them outside. We can't stay away. We watch them swarm on Tory like bees.

"They're like actors on a hospital programme," whispers Beth. "It's like being in *Casualty*."

"It's scary," says Sameena. "What if she really is dead? I've never seen a dead person before."

The paramedics test her pulse. They stick something down her throat for oxygen and plug her into a machine.

"Is she dead?" asks Jess again.

"No," says a paramedic, "she's not dead, but she's seriously injured and we need to get her to hospital as soon as we can. Are you Mum?" he asks, looking at Georgie.

"Yes," says Georgie. "I mean, no. I'm Jess's mum. Tory's here for a sleepover." She casts her hand over us.

"They all are. They were having fun and… I don't know what happened!"

Another paramedic brings a stretcher. They lift Tory on and clip her to a special thing to keep her head straight, then they carry her through the back gate to the ambulance.

Sameena runs along next to her. "Get better soon, Tory," she says. "We love you."

Beth waves. I'm still frozen with shock. I can't believe what just happened.

Jess's eyes are glassy and wide. "She still might die, you know," she says. "We might have to do an interview with the police and be on the telly."

Georgie paces around the garden. She holds her head in her hands. She stabs the grass with her spiky high heels.

"Thank God she's not dead," she repeats over and over again. "Thank God she's not dead!" She turns to Jess. "Your father's going to be furious when he finds out about this. We're both going to be in BIG trouble."

Jess closes in on herself. "It wasn't *my* fault," she says. She casts her eyes round the garden. "It was…"

"Will you be coming with us, madam?" a paramedic asks.

"Yes! No!" she says, looking at us. "I can't leave this lot alone. I need to drop them all off home, then go to Tory's parents. OH! MY! GOD! How am I going to explain this to them?" She looks at the man. "I'll go and tell them, then bring them along."

When the ambulance pulls away, silence drapes a heavy black cloak over us. I creep around the garden and gather up my things.

"This wasn't supposed to happen," shrieks Georgie, looking at us all. "WHAT ON EARTH WAS GOING ON?"

Sameena and Beth are silent; their heads droop low with shame.

"Tell me, Jemima," says Georgie, "why exactly were you naked?"

Jess slips into the shadows. Slides into the dark.

"We were playing Truth or Dare," I say. My voice wobbles, like a small wriggling mouse is caught in my throat. "And Tory dared me to shower in freezing cold water. And then when I was in the shower everyone stole all the towels and my clothes and started throwing them out the window so I couldn't get dressed."

"Is this right?" Georgie asks, looking at the others, swivelling her head from one to the next. Then, without waiting for their answer, she signals for me to continue.

"And then Tory was dangling my knickers out of the window..." My voice cracks, sharp diamond tears nip my eyes. "And then... and then... I suddenly thought... and then..."

"And then you said..." says Jess, stepping into the light. "You said, 'I hate you, Tory Halligan and I wish you were dead.' And that was when you pushed her."

Her words fall from her mouth like dangerous rocks and everyone's eyes crush me.

"*What?*" shrieks Georgie.

"That was when she pushed her," repeats Jess.

Chapter 18

She avoids my gaze...

Back at home the wind whips around the house. Mum's eyes brew like thunder. The Bean screams his head off for his midnight feed. Milo snoozes in his bed and Granny's in the kitchen making tea.

"I need you to go through it again, Jemima," says Mum. "Tell me exactly what happened, just one more time. So it's straight in my head."

"I didn't do it, Mum," I say. "I promise you! It was an accident. It was *them* in the wrong. *They* were teasing *me*! They made me freeze in the shower, then they threw my things out of the window."

"This is the bit I don't understand," says Mum. "Why

189

in heaven's name would they do that? You were having a sleepover. Sleepovers are supposed to be fun!"

"It's your fault," I say, "for not believing me. I told you they hated me. They only invited me because you *asked* if I could go!"

My words slap my mum's face. Her cheeks bloom red.

"I was just…" she says, "you know…"

"It was so embarrassing, Mum. Jess told me what you did and I felt so stupid!"

Her eyes move around the room, avoiding my gaze. She nibbles her nails.

"So, if Jess is telling the truth you would have a motive then?" she sighs. "They were being mean to you… so… It's not uncommon to want revenge, sweetheart. But this is taking it a bit far, Mima! And what's all this stuff Jess is saying about death threats? Did you really say you wanted Tory to die?"

I break open like a wave. Salty tears roll down my cheeks. I need a hug, but I'm too scared to ask. I need my dad!

"I did *say* it," I cry, "but I didn't *mean* it. I promise! I was upset and angry. I didn't expect *this* to happen."

"Well, what did you think might happen if you're messing about near open windows, Mima?" She slumps down on the sofa and groans. "I would have thought you were all old enough to know better!"

I can't tell her I'd decided to jump. I can't say I needed to fly. I can't say anything. Everyone would think I was mad.

"I wish Dad would call," I say. "He'd believe me. He'd know what to do."

Mum makes a little gasp. Her hand flies to her mouth. She fiddles with her lips.

"Oh, Mima, sweetheart, I'm so, so sorry..." she whispers. "With all the fuss about Tory and everything I completely forgot to tell you that he called this afternoon while you were at Jess's. He sent his love, Mima, and he's OK. He's well. But I'm truly sorry you didn't get to speak to him."

"I knew it!" I say. "I *said* he'd call!" My eyes start swimming with tears. "I need to talk to him so badly, Mum, and if only you hadn't made me go!"

My tears spill over and run down my cheeks. I need my dad so much.

Mum lifts her arms up to hug me, but I pull away.

I don't want her. I want my dad! I take a sharp breath in and glare at her. It's all her fault!

Heat, the colour of hate, rises up my spine.

"I told you I didn't want to go to the stupid sleepover in the first place and now because of *you* everything's gone wrong. I'm going to bed," I say. "I don't want to talk any more."

Mum runs her hands through her hair. Her eyes look tired and grey.

"Mima, sweetheart," she says, "I need you to think really hard about what exactly happened at Jess's tonight. We want to get the facts right before we go into the details with Tory's parents, so Jess and Georgie are coming back in the morning to talk. I'm so worried about it all, about you and everything and we just need to get this straight!"

I can't sleep, not for hours and hours and hours. Tory's eyes flash in mine. Her terror squeezes my chest. I didn't mean for her to fall. I replay the whole thing a thousand million times and on every replay the picture changes. Sometimes I'm an angel about to fly, my white wings ruffling in the wind, the bright moon shining in front of me. Then sometimes all I see are both of us scuffling on the window ledge and me giving her an extra little nudge. The problem is that it all happened so fast. How will anyone ever know the truth? I thought I'd tried to push her back inside. I was the one who wanted to fall. But why would Jess say I pushed her if it wasn't really true?

My mind skips to my dad and missing his call. I can't believe I wasn't here. We get one half-hour-long call each week and so far I've missed them both! All the other weeks the communication systems have been down. It's rubbish. My life is rubbish. My poor dad probably had to stand there in the baking heat listening to Milo going on and on about *Toy Story 3*. Then Mum whining about sleepless nights with the Bean and Granny telling him to eat his green vegetables. At least *I* would have had a proper conversation with him. *We* would have talked about interesting and wonderful things.

Tory Halligan's still moon face looms again like a big round cheese in my eyes. She haunts my sleep, she creeps me out. I've never seen a near-dead person before. Her utter silence was like a sting. And it might have been me all twisted on the ground. Dread thumps the dark corners inside me. What if I had died? What then?

Where would I be right now? Would I be a ghost yet, or a shadow or an angel floating above everyone, looking down? Would everyone be crying for me?

My own near-dead face dangles in front of my eyes. Then Dad's. Red blood on yellow sand. I can't breathe. I squeeze my leg hard. I slap my cheek. I pinch my arm. I need to make sure I'm alive. I might've been an angel, but I don't want to die!

My biro angels have faded from the shower. I find my pens and ink them in, then set their brilliance free. A million white flashes through the twinkling night. Then Tory's twisted leg smashes into my brain. The black-silhouetted tree creaks and cracks and *Stinky knickers! Stinky knickers! Stinky knickers!* clashes like cymbals in my ears.

I creep along the hallway to Granny's room. She's fast asleep with her mouth wide open. She's snoring to the stars. I stand and watch her for a while. She looks like a chicken. Puckered skin sags round her mouth. Coarse grey hairs sprout from her chin. I imagine her as a little girl with red apple cheeks and sparkling eyes, all alone in the world because of angry people with bombs. I'm scared to wake her in case I make her jump.

Granny's had too many things make her jump in her life.

The Bean screams his head off again in Mum's room. Mum sighs and swears under her breath.

I pull Granny's cover back. I nudge her over and slide inside.

It's warm in here, close to Granny. And Granny is a miracle because although she's fast asleep her wrinkly hand searches for mine. We link our fingers and hold on tight.

Chapter 19

My eyes search hers for the truth...

When the sun peeps its head over the horizon and the early morning mist still hovers on the grass, Granny brings us in some tea. She pumps up our pillows and settles us both down. I wonder if Granny misses Grandpa in her bed? If every morning she wakes up and expects to find him there, and every day it's a shock when she remembers he's dead? I wonder if when she held my hand last night a faded old memory inside her thought my hand was his?

Or maybe her hand spends the nights searching for a small boy named Derek with a solemn face and big soft eyes.

We sit and sip our tea in silence. Then Granny speaks.

"Must have been a shock, I 'spect, watching that friend of yours fall and everything."

I take another sip.

"She's not my friend, Granny," I whisper. "She's mean. She made me do this Dare game. I had to have a freezing cold shower and she threw my clothes out of the window."

Granny looks at me with the same piercing eyes she uses on my dad.

"Are you sure you didn't give her an extra little push then, Jemima?" she asks. "You know, without thinking, like. Just to get her back?"

My eyes search hers for the truth.

"Because you'd better get your story straight, pet," she says. "Once and for all, see, before that Georgie woman comes over and starts talking. She's a gossip that one."

I rerun the whole of yesterday afternoon in my head. Me not wanting to go. The cinema. Ned. The pizza. Me drawing Dad's angels and then the Truth or Dare game. Everything is clear, except for that bit. I can

197

remember all the tiny details, but the Truth or Dare sticks in my throat.

"I remember feeling panicked," I say, "when they started throwing all the towels out the window. Then Jess and Tory Halligan got into such a frenzy they started on my clothes."

"Slow it down, pet," she says, gently taking hold of my hand. "Bit by bit. That's what you have to do with things when you're not so sure."

"Well, they were teasing me," I say. "I was like piggy-in-the-middle, and Tory Halligan started flapping my clothes and stuff out in the wind and letting them go, one by one."

"And then?" asks Granny.

"And then she had my knickers," I say. "That's it, she had my knickers and she was shouting 'Stinky knickers, stinky knickers', and I couldn't bear it, Granny. I was all naked and she made me feel so... so... low. Do you know what I mean?"

She nods and waves me on with her hand.

"Then I started reaching for them, and she pulled and stretched further and further away and then we both pulled and stretched and we started to topple and

198

the shampoo went everywhere and... I remember now..."

I see myself standing on the window ledge. Waiting to fly. My feathers ruffle in the wind. Stars twinkle in the night.

"We looked at each other," I continue. "We both knew we were about to fall and then..."

I take another sip of tea and squeeze Granny's hand hard, like if I don't I'll somehow fall out of myself and tumble to the ground.

"And then...?" she prompts.

Tears well in my eyes and plop like sparkling diamonds on my cheeks.

I look at Granny. Her eyes hold me tight, willing me to dig right down to the truth.

"The truth will set you free, pet," she says. "See, either way, whatever happens, it's the most important thing. You know what you're dealing with once you've got the truth in your hands, out on the plate, so to speak, for everyone to see."

"It's so hard, Granny," I say.

I wish I were brave enough to tell the absolute truth. I wish I were brave enough to stand on the bed and say,

GRANNY, I WAS ABOUT TO JUMP OUT OF THE WINDOW! I THOUGHT I COULD FLY! I THOUGHT I WAS AN ANGEL! I THOUGHT I COULD BRING DAD BACK HOME!

Ned's right. How could I be so dumb? So stupid? What was I thinking?

"I didn't push her out of the window," I say. "I know that for sure. I tried to push her back inside, but never out. There, that's the truth. It was an accident, I promise."

"So you didn't push her then?" says Granny, checking one last time.

"I didn't push her," I say. "I'm sure of it now."

Like someone has drawn a line under a story and written *The End*, Granny gets up sharp and tips me out of bed.

"Off to the shower with you," she says, pulling her dressing gown on. "Then downstairs smart, we've got pancakes to make and lessons to learn."

By the time I get downstairs Granny's made an Everest of pancakes and Milo's already tucking in.

"Sit down, Jemima," she says, "and tell me exactly *why* you let these girls treat you so badly? Where's your backbone gone, pet?"

My eyes settle on the floor. How do I explain that Tory Halligan turns me to milk?

"Because if I'm right," Granny smiles, "you're a Taylor-Jones, is that correct?"

I nod. I squeeze lemon on my pancake and dribble a spiral of maple syrup from a spoon.

"And us Taylor-Joneses," she says, "have backbone, see, lots of it! How do you think I managed when my world crumbled to dust? I didn't have anyone on this earth to run to, Jemima. I was nine years old and completely alone in the world. There were plenty of folk out there ready to take advantage of me, but I wasn't having any of it. That's 'cause I had backbone, see. I learned to take care of myself. There was one big girl in school when I was first evacuated to Wales who had me pinned up against the wall with her fists curled up tight. Her teeth clenched and grinding in my ears. But believe you me, Jemima, even *she* didn't get the better of me. Think on it now, if I hadn't been able to take care of myself I'd have been dead long before now, pet, and you might not even have been born."

I stir my hot chocolate and drink in her words.

"I sometimes wish I'd never been born," I say. "It would have been easier for everyone."

Granny slams her mug on the table and shoots me with her glare.

"Don't ever let me hear you say such a thing again," she snaps. "Do you understand? This is a precious life we've been given, Jemima. It's yours to make the most of. You can't go blaming others for making it grim or go about wishing you were dead. You've got to pick it up with both hands, pet, and treasure it. You've got to learn to take care of it. Life's a gift, see, a truly beautiful gift."

Granny sits close to me. I feel her gentle breath on my cheek.

"But I don't know how!" I say.

"Well, that's what most people find difficult, pet," she says. "You see, most people think taking care of yourself is about buckling up. About being strong, about shutting people out and pretending things don't hurt when they do. Most people hold their feelings in for a long time. They build great walls round their hearts. But then you see, pet, just like the little piggies in the story, if you've built up great walls round yourself it only

202

takes someone like Tory Whatshername to come along and blow them all down."

She sips her tea.

"The real problem, pet," she says, "is that you're still not trusting life. You're still trying to make things happen your way. I can see it in your eyes."

She takes another sip.

"Trust yourself to tell Tory Whatshername how you feel. Tell your teachers how you feel. Tell your mum. Trusting life, Mima, starts with trusting yourself. Trusting yourself to see the truth of the matter. Because underneath all that tallywash you're quite wise, you know. You know what you need to do."

Milo is eating his seventh pancake. Mum is on her way downstairs with the Bean.

"You see, pet," she whispers, "the problem with walls is that it might mean people can't get in and hurt you, but it also means you can't get out. It means you're stuck inside yourself. All alone! And that's such a lonely place to be. So stay close to the truth," she says, "and that will connect your heart to the rest of the world. Then never ever stray. That's true power, pet."

Granny tucks my hair behind my ear.

"That's better," she says. "Now I can see that pretty face of yours. I want you to promise me, Jemima, that you'll never let anyone bully you ever again. Not ever! If it starts to happen, then remember your backbone. Promise?"

I nod.

"Well, Bex," says Granny when Mum comes up to the table, "she says she didn't do it, it was an accident and I believe her. We've got to believe her, see, that's what family's for."

My mum's eyes shift around the room. She stands behind Milo with one arm resting on his back and the other cradling the Bean. She has no arms left for me and doubt wipes across her face like a smear.

"Well, I'm sorry," she says, as if I'm not even in the room listening to the conversation, "but I'm confused. Why would Jess say such a thing if it weren't true?" She throws me a look full of bombs. "I love you, Mima, so much, but something doesn't fit. Something's not quite right."

I shrink away from her and hide behind my wall.

Granny chips in. "Backbone! Jemima, pet, where's your backbone?"

I sip my chocolate. I draw my eyes up to Mum's.

"I *am* telling the truth," I say, "and it feels like you don't believe me. It doesn't feel right because it's Jess who's telling lies."

Granny's eyes shine. She pats my hand. And that is lovely, but I need a pat from my mum. I wish she'd leave the boys for a moment to come and comfort me.

But she won't. Her ears are made of cloth. Her eyes are full of fire.

"I don't know," she says, latching the Bean on to her breast. "You've been acting so weird lately, Jemima. All that pretending to be ill and everything. I don't know who or what to believe. One of you is telling lies, that's for sure. And it's a serious matter. A girl's life is on the line."

Her words slice through my chest. I run to Dad's wardrobe and build a deep, thick wall round my heart. I pull his red and gold mess dress jacket on to my knees. I breathe in his smell and hold him tight.

"I wish you were here, Dad," I whisper. "I'm so scared."

Chapter 20

I know what I did...

When Georgie and Jess arrive, Mum acts all serious. She makes coffee and opens the packet of shortbread biscuits she keeps in the cupboard for special occasions. She zips herself in and keeps her lips tight. Her hands tremble when she pours. Her eyes twitch in her skull.

"I phoned the hospital this morning," says Georgie, "and Tory's stable, thank God. They think she's going to be OK. They won't know for sure until they've done the brain scan and stuff to check for more serious damage, but so far so good." Georgie glares at me. "She's in a *coma*! Her family are at her bedside waiting for her to *wake up*! Can you imagine what *that* must be like? And then there's her leg. That was broken, of course! We could all see that."

She leans her head in towards Mum's. So close their fringes touch.

"It was *terrible*, Bex," she whispers, "thinking I had a dead child in my back garden. OH! MY! GOD! It was awful! I'm still reeling from the shock. I'm dreading Tom finding out. He'll go *mad*!"

Jess is on the sofa. Her knees tucked under her chin. She sip, sips her juice and keeps her eyes down low. Every so often she slides them in my direction and sends me a black look full of hate. I'd like to throw bombs in her face and watch her explode. Mrs Bostock would understand that Jess wouldn't be telling such a lie if she were a happy child. She would try to get to the bottom of things and find out what's eating Jess's heart. She would pop chocolates in her pocket. But I don't care about Jess. I wish I could stand up on the sofa and say, JESS, WILL YOU JUST OPEN YOUR FAT MOUTH AND TELL EVERYONE THE TRUTH SO THAT I CAN GET ON WITH MY LIFE! But I don't. I just sit there. I press my finger in the tiny sugar crystals on the biscuit plate, then stick it in my mouth and let them melt on my tongue.

"Well, what are we going to do?" says Mum. "How can we solve this?"

She looks at me, then at Jess.

We both look away.

"I know what I saw!" says Jess.

"I know what happened," I say. "It was an accident! She lost her balance and I tried to pull her back in."

"I mean," says Georgie, "if you did do it, Mima, then we really have to let Tory's parents know and then they might press charges. I don't want to scare you or anything, but it's a terrible thing to do. It's a crime. You can't go pushing people out of windows willy-nilly, just because you don't like the game you're playing."

Dragon spikes rise on my skin. Lion's teeth grow in my head. Sharp claws sprout from under my nails. I'd like to scratch her face. I'd like to stand up and say, I DIDN'T DO IT, YOU STUPID WOMAN, DON'T YOU KNOW? IN FACT, I WAS TRYING TO JUMP OUT OF THE WINDOW MYSELF. I WAS TRYING TO FLY THROUGH YOUR TREES! But I don't because I can't tell the truth because everyone will think that I'm mad.

But I do come up with an idea.

"Let's wait for Tory to wake up," I say. "She'll say the same as me."

"Might not," says Jess. "She might have lost her memory. She might end up as a vegetable and have to be in care for ever and ever. She might never walk again! Or see! Or hear! That might be *it* for her!"

"Jess is right," says Georgie. "That might be *it* for poor Tory!"

Mum drops her head in her hands. She sighs and says, "Let's go through it one more time."

So we do. Jess goes first. Then me.

"But I'm still not any clearer about what actually happened," says Mum, when we've finished speaking. "We'll just have to wait for Tory to wake up and see what she has to say."

"But shouldn't we talk to the police?" says Jess. "If we suspect Jemima of attempted murder we have to let them know."

Granny storms into the kitchen with the Bean tucked under her arm. Milo trails along behind.

"I've heard quite enough of this gossip," she snaps. "The child says she's innocent. So leave her be."

Granny's words slap everyone into silence.

209

When Georgie and Jess have gone, Granny mutters under her breath, "Little minx, that one. Little minx." And I agree.

I go upstairs to do some work on my presentation. I open my laptop and Google *Derek – Canada – Blitz*. But it's rubbish. All Google comes up with is stuff about football. I slam the lid down. I kick my bed. Without Derek, my presentation is going to be as rubbish as me. Even Callum Richardson's boring one on football is going to be better than mine.

The trouble is that it's all so clear in my head. I'm standing up at the front of the class with a clear crystal voice to make Dad proud. And I'm focused, focused, focused, and my picture boards are propped up on display. And then I click the button and my film of Granny comes on. She tells her story. She's crying because she's so upset about the fact that her soul mate slipped through her fingers. Then the film moves on to one of Derek. He's sitting there all old in his chair, telling us how tragic his life has been because he lost his one true love. Then I click my fingers and a flock of white, white doves flies through the room like a million angels. Some romantic music starts up and not an eye in the classroom is dry and Mrs Cassidy has called Mrs Bostock to the room to join us because she thinks my presentation is truly brilliant. And then for my grand finale the doors crash open and in walk Granny and Derek arm in arm with love hearts floating all around them and pink roses in their arms. And then everybody cheers and Derek asks Granny to marry him and Granny says yes. And then they ask me if I want to be a bridesmaid. And I say yes. And everything is perfect! And I get an A******** for my good work.

I pull out the camcorder and plug the USB lead into my laptop. Even if I don't have Derek, I have the film of Milo being an evacuee and if I can make one of Granny at least I'll have something to show. I've seen Dad do it a million times before. It's easy. All he does is click a few buttons and edit a few frames and he gets a perfect film. I put my sunglasses on and pretend I'm a real film-maker making an important documentary programme for TV. I think I'm going to like this job.

And then a box pops up telling me I need to install some special software. I don't have a clue about software and Mum won't have a clue and neither will Granny.

I have to face facts. My presentation is going to be

rubbish. I should have done it on dog rescue homes or Walt Disney.

Ned is right. There are a million things I can't make happen. If I were twenty-five years old things might be better. I'd have learned all about film-making. I'd know all about software. I'd be able to say NO to things I don't want to do. Twelve is confusing. Twelve is rubbish. Just like me. I'll have to make do with the photo of Milo dressed up as Derek.

I did do *that* on my own. At least *that* is good.

I pull out the USB lead and throw the camcorder in its bag.

If Granny and Derek were supposed to find each other then they would have done it themselves. Fate would have pulled them together like magnets from the opposite sides of the world. The flow of life would have caught them on its tide.

I pull out my presentation boards and sigh. They're flat and boring and do not speak of love. They don't feel like broken hearts. They won't make people cry. I stroke the photo of Milo dressed up as Derek and whisper, "Where are you, Derek Bach?" I pull back my sleeve and flick an angel into the air. He starts flying off to Dad. I whistle him back just in time and send him off to Derek. "Go find him! Please?"

I stroke the photo of my great-grandparents. I whisper to them, "What happened to you all? Where are you now? Where do you go when you die?" They stare back at me with their stupid sunshine smiles. I wonder if their smiles would have been so big if they'd known their bodies were going to end up strewn all over the rubble like shrapnel. I don't think so. I think they might have run for their lives. I flick an angel to them and a gorgeous one to baby Joan. They fly so white through my window, so radiant to the faraway place I can never know of until I die.

Then I send a million angels to Dad. So bright they hurt my eyes. "Please bring him back to me!"

I glue sparkles and sprinkles and hearts over my rain-grey boards and make a big swish of red and silver hearts from Dad to me. I stroke his face. It's a photo I took of him just before he left. We'd gone for a walk. Just him and me. To talk about things. I snapped it when he wasn't looking.

I kiss my finger, then plant the kiss on his cheek and I wish a flower would grow.

If Ned were talking to me I'd go and see him. I'd randomly knock on his door and say "Hi!" And I wouldn't take a guitar because I don't have one, but maybe I'd make up the lyrics to a song. Maybe Ned and me could make a band. Maybe his gramps really could help me find Derek.

But I can't do that. I'm not brave. And anyway Ned hates me.

Granny pops her head round the door.

"Here, pet," she says, putting a sandwich and drink next to me on the floor. "Thought you might be hungry."

"Thanks, Granny," I say. "I do love you!"

She smiles and kisses the top of my head.

"Granny?" I say. "I can't make the film of you because I don't know how all Dad's stuff works, so I wondered… if you'd maybe consider… coming into my school on presentation day to tell everyone what happened to you in the Blitz and all about Derek and everything?"

Granny plops down on my bed.

"I don't think so, pet," she says. "I don't think anyone's going to be interested in listening to an old fogey like me. Oh, Jemima," she says, stroking my hair, "my little Sherlock Holmes. Forget about it all. It's in the past. It's gone. Forget about Derek, pet. You finding his photo is plenty enough for me. And anyway, Mum's really not happy with all this war obsession. Perhaps you should think of something different to do your presentation on."

When Granny leaves, I shove my stupid presentation stuff away. I pull my gas mask on and lie on my bed, my magic bed that will fly me far away from here.

Chapter 21

Lonely is the emptiest place in the world...

No one is talking to me. But the Tory Halligan coma story is the topic on everyone's lips. The school is buzzing with it. On Monday morning Mrs Bostock drags me into her room.

"Do you need to talk, Jemima?" she says, filling my fist with chocolate. "Because I'm here to listen if there's anything you need to say. General reports are that you're doing well, but I'm concerned. This Tory Halligan thing – were you involved?"

I pop a chocolate in my mouth. I shake my head. I can't tell Mrs Bostock the truth about anything, let alone what happened with Tory. If I were to tell her the truth about something, I'd stand on her chair and say, MRS BOSTOCK, I HATE COMING TO YOUR SCHOOL EVERY DAY BECAUSE IT TRULY IS THE MOST BORING, BORING PLACE IN THE WORLD AND I'M LEAVING YOUR OFFICE AND GOING HOME NOW AND I'M NEVER COMING BACK! GOODBYE! And then I'd walk out of the school gates without looking back and my life would become much more wonderful than it is right now.

On Monday afternoon Ned comes up to me and says, "Now I've lost all respect for you, Jemima. That was a sick thing to do."

I just stand there and don't say one word to defend myself.

Hayley, Sameena and Beth keep clinging on to Jess. Without Tory stitching them together they're lost. Jess is the new queen. I think she'd like us all to bow down to her and curtsey. But I won't. She glared at me on the bus on Tuesday and flurried everyone to the back seat, far, far away from me.

I hate Jess.

Jess hates me.

That's how it's always been, but we've never been brave enough to say.

Tory Halligan is still in a coma. She won't wake up and I don't blame her. She's probably having much more fun in her coma dreams. Why would she want to wake up to this world?

After games on Wednesday Jess whispers in my ear, "She still might die, you know, and it'll all be your fault."

After double science she sends me a text. Pip. Pip. *More bombs. Ur dad might die too. U might never see him again. I hate you, Jemima.*

Images from war films race screaming through my mind and I worry about my dad. *Please be OK, Dad! Please, please be OK!*

Every day I eat lunch on my own. It tastes like cardboard. No one sits near me. No one speaks to me. Anyone would think I had a deathly contagious disease. I'd like to stand up on the table and say, EXCUSE ME, BUT I AM NOT RESPONSIBLE FOR TORY HALLIGAN'S COMA, OR HER NEAR DEATH. I AM NOT A MURDER SUSPECT. IT WAS AN ACCIDENT. IT IS SUPPOSED TO BE ME LYING THERE NEARLY DEAD. NO ONE WOULD

NOTICE IF I WERE GONE, AND FOR YOUR INFORMATION I WOULDN'T MISS ANY OF YOU ONE BIT! But I don't. I munch on my cardboard salad instead.

People point and whisper at me because of Jess and her spiteful gossiping tongue. Rumours spread like butter.

I thought I knew what lonely was.

But I didn't.

I do now.

Lonely is the emptiest place in the world, the place where love is banned.

Every night when I get home from school my mum pats me on the head, like I'm a dog and says, "Go on up and get on with your prep, sweetheart. Dinner will be ready soon."

She edges round me, scared I'll go off like a bomb. She doesn't know what to believe. For once she is lost for words.

Granny fluffs around me. She stuffs me full of pancakes. She pats my arm. She irons my clean washing with extra-special care. She stacks it on my bed and leaves a flower on the top of the pile. Milo roars about the place. He bashes into me. One day he scratches my arm by accident with the tip of a metal plane. Tears sting my eyes. I squeeze them back in. I have no time for sharp diamonds now.

On Friday night I lift the Bean from his Moses basket and take him outside to marvel at the stars. They twinkle down on us like silver rain.

"There's The Plough," I say, "and Orion's Belt."

And then I can't show him any more because I feel too sad. Stars remind me of our dad.

"Life is a mysterious thing, little Bean," I say.

And then I show him the angels on my arms and we blow them through the sky together. They rise from the inky blue to a white flash of wonder, a flurry of love, an incandescent blaze through the night. I tell the Bean where they're going because he doesn't understand about places like Afghanistan yet.

"One day you will," I say, "when you're a bigger beautiful boy and you might like tanks and trunks like Milo or you might become a pacifist like Ned. You might play the guitar like John Lennon and wear laces on your shoes that look like vines."

Ned creeps uninvited into my thoughts too often.

His halo hair shimmers in my eyes. His sapphire eyes pierce my mind. I push him away.

I grab a fistful of stars and sprinkle them in the Bean's eyes.

"Little Bean, I wish for you to grow strong and brave and healthy," I say, "and for you to have a truly happy and wonderful life and for you to marry a beautiful princess and live happily ever after."

I'm the good fairy really, not the wicked one.

On Saturday morning, when my ears have almost given up stretching, the phone rings.

It's my dad!

I wait and wait while Mum natters on about rubbish. I wait and wait while Milo tells Dad about his game. I wait and wait while Granny makes sure he's drinking enough water. And then it's my turn.

"Daddy!" I say.

The line is crackly, but the sound of his voice melts me into a bubble of love. It wraps its arms round me and gently soothes my heart. It's like I'm there in the desert, next to my dad and my dad is next to me. Holding tightly on to my hand.

I have so many things to say. I don't know where to

start. I need his help with Derek. I need to tell him about Tory and about me wanting to fly.

"Dad!" I say again.

Then Mum steps in front of me and flaps her arms wildly in my face. She shakes her head. She whispers, "Don't say anything about Tory, I don't want him to worry! Georgie doesn't want Jess's dad to know. Don't say anything about anything at all. OK? Just talk about nice things."

All my worries jam in my throat. Dad says, "Love you, Mima, sweetheart." Then he says, "Knock, knock." And I croak, "Who's there?" and he says, "Army," and I squeak, "Army who?" And he says, "Are me and you still going for ice cream?"

I try to make a laugh sound. I do. But it's a struggle to cover up the tears that are rolling down my cheeks and choke in my throat.

"I miss you, Dad," I squeak. "Please come home soon."

His time is up.

He says, "Bye-bye, sweet girl." And the phone goes dead.

I turn to Mum.

"I need to go and see Tory," I say.

"Really?" says Mum. She rests her chin on her hand. She thinks for a while and says, "That's the most sensible and bravest thing you've said all week, Jemima."

We're silent in the car. We're busy thinking. Mum pulls over to a petrol station and hops out to buy red grapes and flowers.

"She won't be able to eat them," I say. "If she's still in the coma she won't be able to eat."

Mum snaps, "That's not the point, Mima. That's not the point and you know it. Why do you always have to be so difficult. God help me when you're a teenager."

Once the Bean is out of his car seat and strapped safely in his sling we look for signs to intensive care.

"That way," says Mum, pointing. Then she's off like a whirlwind. She pushes through the doors. She marches up the stairs.

A sharp lump sticks in my throat. My legs feel like milk.

"Mum," I say, having second thoughts about coming, "Mum... we don't even know if we're welcome. Maybe

223

we should have called. Tory Halligan doesn't exactly *like* me, you know? I'm only here because I need to find out. I need to know…"

"What d'you mean?" says Mum. "Why wouldn't we be welcome? Why ever wouldn't she like you? I know she got carried away with the Truth and Dare game you all played… but, well… I'm sure you all got a bit high spirited. But it's important to remember, Mima, that it was a game, nothing more. I'm sure she didn't really mean you any harm."

I sigh.

"And anyway," she smiles, "they must have liked you to have invited you along in the first place."

"Only because you asked if I could go. Remember?"

Mum furrows her brow, then smoothes away the lines. She fans her face.

"Of course she likes you, Jemima, and if it was an accident, like you say, then there's nothing to worry about. You're just too sensitive, sweetheart, that's your problem. You need to give them more of a chance to get to know you. That's how you'll make friends."

When we get to intensive care, the doors to the ward are locked. Mum shakes them furiously, demanding to be let in. A buzzer at the side of the door goes off and an invisible voice speaks.

"Can I help you?"

"Er... erm..." says Mum. "We've come to see Victoria Halligan. She was admitted last week."

"Are you family?" asks the voice. "I'm afraid only close relatives are allowed."

"Well, no," says Mum, looking at me like I know what to do next. "But my daughter, here – Jemima – she's a school friend and we'd very much like to pop in. Just a few minutes will do. Just to say a quick hello."

"I'm afraid it definitely won't be possible for your daughter to come in," says the voice. "Children aren't allowed. Stay there, I'll speak to Mrs Halligan."

After a few minutes Mrs Halligan pushes through the door.

"Hello?" she says, looking puzzled. "Can I help?"

"We've come to see how Victoria is doing," says Mum, zipping herself into her thick skin and poshing up her voice. "You know Jemima – she's a school friend of Victoria's. She was at the sleepover. We wanted to bring her these."

Mum shoves the flowers and grapes into Mrs Halligan's hands.

"Well, thank you," says Mrs Halligan. She looks at me. "I haven't heard of you before, Jemima, but it's lovely to meet you. Lovely you both took the trouble to come, really it is. It's been a difficult week," she says. "You know, she's still... and I'm afraid I can't invite you in... it's only... you know... family."

"Of course," says Mum, blood rising like a sunrise in her cheeks. "We'll leave you to it... hope Victoria... hope..."

My heart dips in my chest. I need to talk to Tory. I need her to wake up. We need to come up with a plan. No one must know what I tried to do because I'm not mad, really I'm not. I think Mum's right, I think I'm just unhinged!

Chapter 22

My words bite her...

On Monday lunchtime I go to the IT room and Google *The Salvation Army*. There was an article in the Sunday paper that said they're good at finding missing people.

A flurry of excitement bubbles in my chest. Maybe this is it.

The end of my search.

I dial the number.

"Hello," says the lady on the end of the phone.

"Hi," I say, "I'm trying to find someone my granny knew in the war and I wonder if you can help?"

"You have to download the forms from the internet," she says, "and fill them in. We need the person's full name, date of birth and last known address. Without these we can't help, I'm afraid."

"Oh," I say. "I don't have any of those. OK, sorry for troubling you."

I kick the door and throw my phone in my bag.

Maybe I'll be sick on presentation day and have to stay at home.

On the way to drama, Callum Richardson skids up to me.

"Have you heard?" he says.

I shake my head. "No one's talked to me all week, Callum. I haven't heard anything."

"It's Ned," he says. "His gramps just died!"

Sharp claws grab my insides. They twist and squeeze.

"What?" I say. "How? Why? Where's Ned now?"

"Don't know," says Callum. "He has to go to foster care. He doesn't have any other family."

The floor spins out of control. I think I might faint. I'm sorry for Ned, but I'm also sorry for me. Ned said his gramps might be able to help. He said he might know about Derek. If Tory wasn't in a coma and I hadn't made Ned mad then I might have found Derek by now.

My presentation might not have been so bad. I pinch myself. *Stop being so selfish, Jemima, and think of someone else for a change! Think of Ned and his gramps!*

Jess joins us. Her eyes shine.

"Ned's gramps is dead," she says. "He had a stroke. Pop! Just like that. Gone! My mum found out this morning and she said you never know what's going to happen. One minute he was eating his breakfast, then pop! Gone! Now Ned's an orphan. Imagine that."

I glare at Jess and before I can stop myself I open up my mouth and speak. I've had enough of her. At last!

"WHY DON'T YOU JUST SHUT YOUR FAT FACE UP FOR ONE SECOND, JESS," I say. "YOU AND YOUR MUM ARE GETTING ON MY NERVES! YOU ARE LIKE GOSSIPING VAMPIRES WHO FEED ON OTHER PEOPLE'S LIVES!"

My words bite her. She pulls back.

"Me, getting on *your* nerves?" she snaps. "Funny that. I thought it was the other way round. You and your goody-goody life! You and your perfect dad and your perfect mum and your perfect granny who's always fluffing around making pancakes! You and your perfect sweet Milo and your cootchy baby Bean! You and your stupid, stupid angels! You get on my nerves, Jemima Taylor-Jones, more than anyone else on this planet. Even more than my horrible dad!"

Tears spring in her eyes.

"You think you have a bad time?" she says. "You want to try living in my life for a while, Jemima, then you'd know what bad really is."

Her shoulders judder with sadness.

"It's hard being me," she says. "It's hard being twelve. No one understands and I know you're a freak and everything, but apart from that you have everything a girl would ever want. You've got it all, Jemima Taylor-Jones, and I have nothing."

I take a breath. I'm full of shock.

"I didn't choose my family, you know," I say. "I don't make them like they are and anyway, whatever my life is like it's no excuse for telling lies. I didn't push Tory and you know it!"

And then I go too far.

"And it's not my fault you have such a crap family."

And that does it. Jess lifts her hand. Her palm swings towards my cheek and the slap sound echoes down the corridor. My hand flies to the sting. My eyes sparkle and flicker with pain. My mouth drops open like an O.

Callum Richardson breaks the silence.

"Fight! Fight! Fight!" he smiles, punching the air with his fist. "And I thought nothing fun ever happened in this school."

Mrs Bostock appears from nowhere, like Nanny McPhee with her stick. She bats Callum out of the way and takes hold of Jess's hand and mine.

"This is a respectable establishment," she says to the walls, "and such things as fighting are Definitely! Not! Allowed!"

When we get to her office, Jess's eyes are wide, searching for Mrs Bostock's torture tools. She's looking for the bones of people who didn't survive, for the abandoned pens of skeletons who have written a million lines.

But I know all that is in Jess's imagination.

I know the truth of what happens in Mrs Bostock's office. I know all she does in here is hand out chocolates and smile.

"Now," she says, "I know life is upsetting for you both at the moment and your families are living on the edge, but really, let's see an end to this warring, shall we? Now, tell me what's going on."

Jess says, "Nothing, Mrs Bostock," and zips her mouth.

I say, "Nothing, Mrs Bostock," and send a million black bombs to Jess.

Mrs Bostock says, giving us each a chocolate, "Well, I'm keeping my eagle eye on both of you. And if this has anything to do with Tory Halligan I'd be grateful if you'd speak up."

Jess and I stare straight ahead without blinking. We're giving nothing away at all.

"Well," says Mrs Bostock, putting the lid on the chocolate tin, "remember, if you feel you need to chat to me or see the counsellor, I'll be happy to arrange it for you."

On our way back to drama Jess's eyes shine.

"She's mad!" she says. "What kind of crazy head teacher hands out chocolates when you've done something wrong? I thought she strung people up and gouged their eyes out!"

I shrug. My fire-alarm secret glows warm deep down inside.

Jess looks at me.

"I really do hate you," she says, "and I hope Tory Halligan does die, then at least we can get rid of you!"

Later that evening Georgie comes over with Jess. I'm up in my room hiding from Mum's evil eye.

"Hi!" Mum's voice sings when she opens the door. "Come on in. So lovely, lovely to see you both!" Her voice trills up the stairs, "Mima, come on down – Jess and Georgie are here for supper and Georgie's got some good news."

"She woke up…" Georgie squeals when I get to the bottom of the stairs. "Just an hour or so ago. Just like that. Just like normal. I spoke to Mrs Halligan and she said Tory opened her eyes and smiled and said, 'I'm hungry,' just like that!! And Mrs Halligan said, 'Oh, I've waited so long for that smile.'" She makes a little skip. "Isn't it exciting? Tory's awake! She's alive! She's still a bit groggy, but she's back!"

Jess fumes by the door. I fume back at her. Jess and I are at war.

"Now at least we can find out the truth," she says, shooting seven hundred eye arrows at me.

At suppertime I sit as far away from Jess as possible. I dig at my pasta. I twist it on my fork. I listen to Georgie blabbing on about what Mrs Halligan had to say. Georgie's mouth is a machine. It doesn't stop moving for hours.

"I just couldn't believe my ears. I was out in the garden, pottering away when the phone rang and it was *her* on the other end. She was ever so nice, Bex; she said she wanted me to be first to know because of how much worry I must be going through. We're going to give Tory a few days to recover a bit, then we're going to pop over, aren't we, Jess? Take her a pressie. Welcome her back."

"And did she mention if Tory said anything?" says Mum. "You know, does she remember... *what happened?*"

Granny slams her wine glass on the table and mouths to me, "Backbone, Jemima, backbone."

I sit up straight. "Tory Halligan will tell the same story as me," I say, "because it's the truth."

Granny smiles.

"Well," says Georgie, ignoring me and glowing with gossip, "I didn't want to ask, not just yet. I thought

234

what with her only just waking up and everything… we should give it a bit of time."

Granny coughs. She stares hard at Mum.

"Well," says Mum, "I agree with Georgie. We need to check with Tory." She turns to me. "It's great she's alive and well, Mima, and if you are telling the truth there won't be a problem. But we need to know for sure. It's only right, sweetheart."

Then Georgie starts blabbing on about Ned.

"Poor lamb!" she says. "Sad story, that one. Just Ned and his gramps! No one else in the world!" She mouths to Mum, "He'll have to go to foster care. Nothing for it. He's got stacks of money though. It's left him a very rich boy!" She brings her voice back up to its normal annoying volume. "I heard all about it in the playground this morning when I dropped Jess off. She missed the bus, you see. We overslept. And I thought it was only fair to spread the word. It's important people should know. *Poor lamb!*"

I slide down in my chair. I hide behind my glass and shoot eye arrows at Jess. I hope Mum never tells Georgie secrets of mine.

Chapter 23

Truth is better than dare...

When the house is quiet and still and the world has gone to bed, the wind whips up a storm. I stare out at the night and will my dad to come back home. Rain spits at my window and owls hoot in the trees. Dark clouds rumble through the stars and in the shadows, leaning against a tree, is a boy. A boy with starlight dancing in halo hair. A boy who's holding a guitar.

I press my face on the glass. Ned? Ned? What is Ned doing *here*?

I race downstairs and open the door.

"Ned?" I say. "What are you doing?"

He lifts his face. His tears are mingled with rain.

"Dunno," he says. "Didn't know where else to go. They took my key." His voice cracks. "I can't even get into my house."

"Come in," I whisper, "but be quiet. Everyone's sleeping."

I find juice and snacks in the kitchen and smuggle Ned upstairs.

"Sorry!" he says, wiping his nose with his hand. "I'm sorry, Jemima Puddleduck. I just—"

I press my finger to his lips to shush him. I hand him some juice. We sit on the floor.

"I heard about your gramps," I say. "I'm sorry he died."

"Oh, don't be," he laughs. "Everyone leaves me. You get used to it in the end."

Ned looks up. His lashes sparkle with diamonds. His cheeks flush pink with grief. I hunt in my brain for words.

"I'm sorry," I say again. "What happened?"

Ned leans against my bed. He rests his head in his hands. His voice whispers.

"We were..." he says. "I can't believe it. We were... sitting there just like normal, eating breakfast and he

237

took a sip of his tea and that was it. He toppled. He was suddenly dead. A stroke! Boof! Gone! And I tried to make him come alive. I willed him to come back."

He stuffs his hand in the packet of crisps and crams some in his mouth. Salt planets settle on his lips.

"His face keeps haunting me," he says. "He looked so scared. So shocked by what was happening. And I couldn't stop it. I couldn't do anything. I felt so useless." He swigs orange juice from the carton. His eyes fill up with tears. "You know, it wouldn't be so bad if I had someone else. It's just me now. I feel so alone."

My heart dips. A lump sticks in my throat.

"I'm sorry, Ned."

"They stuck me in a foster home," he says. "They took me straight there, an hour or so after it happened. But if they think I'm staying they've got another think coming. I skipped out the window."

He rubs his face and drags his long fingers through his golden hair. He pulls a loose thread from his jeans. His laces trail like vines.

He looks up.

"I've got money, you know, loads of it, enough to last me for ever. If I can find someone to take me in

238

the holidays I think I'll go to boarding school. That has to be better than care. The money doesn't mean anything though. It can't give me a hug."

His eyes sparkle.

My heart flaps. I'd like to give Ned a hug, but I'm not sure how. I keep my arms by my side. I close my eyes. I stretch my heart across the space between us and wrap him up in love.

My skin creeps with shame. All my life I've been totally swimming in love, but I've been too blind and obsessed with myself to see it. I've been too deaf to hear it, too dumb to feel it. Even my stressed-out mum loves me. She doesn't often show it and our wires keep getting crossed, but she does love me. I know that's true. And now poor Ned's like Granny – totally left alone.

"I can see why you got cross with me," I say. "I'm a spoiled brat. I've been stupid. I'm sorry."

Ned picks up his guitar. He plays the tune to Kiss Twist's 'A Million Angels' and his music spirals to the moon.

"What will you do now?" I ask.

"The very thing you need to learn to do," he says.

"Trust, Jemima Puddleduck. Trust! Things will work out. They always do."

"I am trying to trust," I say, "but it's so difficult."

"Just takes practice," he says, "like anything else worth learning."

His sapphire eyes meet my gunmetal grey ones and we tie a knot in our gaze.

"You could start practising right now," he smiles. "You could tell me something you've never told anyone else before in your life."

I pull my knees up. I cuddle them with my arms. Truth is better than Dare.

"I'm scared most of the time," I whisper. "I'm scared of the wind. I'm scared of people. I don't know how to make friends. I feel stupid and awkward almost all of the time. Your turn."

"I've never met my dad," says Ned. "I don't even know his name. I wish I had a dad, even if he did go off to war. Your turn."

"I even feel scared sitting here with you," I say. "I feel like I should be doing something interesting to make you like me. Or something mean to push you away. You?"

"When I was four years old," says Ned, "my mum dropped me off at my gramps's house. She said she needed to go and find herself. I thought she was going to the shops. She said she'd be back soon. She promised. She said I had to believe her, I had to trust and I did… why wouldn't I? I waited… and Gramps waited." Ned sniffs. He rubs some mud from his shoe. "You?"

"I wish my dad wasn't in the army," I say. "I hide in his wardrobe. I smell his clothes and steal them and wear them when I want to feel close. I have a gas mask, Ned, like your gramps did. I like it. It makes me feel safe. I don't want my dad to die. You?"

Ned rubs his eyes. He blinks hard. Diamonds spill over his lids.

"I hate crying for her," he says. "It's stupid. I don't mind crying for Gramps, at least he was real, but I don't even remember her, not really. You?"

I hide my face in my hair.

"I've never had a proper friend," I whisper, "except for my dad. You?"

I'm taking down my wall, brick by brick. With Ned. How strange to be here in my room, in the middle of this night, with the wild wind raging outside. Foster

241

people might be looking for him. Someone might be worried. But he's here. Eating crisps. With me.

"And we kept waiting," he says, "and eventually we got a letter to say she was never coming back. She's in India or somewhere. In an ashram. She said she couldn't handle being a mum. That was when Gramps washed his hands of her. It was a double pain, you see: I lost my mum, he lost his daughter. Now he'll never see her again. She left it too late. You?"

"I didn't push Tory out of the window," I say. "I promise you, Ned. You?"

"She never wrote to me," says Ned. "Not once, not ever. She used to write to Gramps, but not me. She must hate me."

He crumples like paper. He draws his knees up to his chest. His shoulders shake with tears.

I slide a little closer. I want to touch his arm. I want to comfort him.

Angels flap in my chest.

"She's out there somewhere," I say. "She's still your mum. Maybe you could find her?"

"Never!" he says with fire in his eyes. "I'm never going to look for her. She made her decision to leave me; she'll have to live with it. I'll survive; I'll be OK. I'll trust life to carry me on its tide. Gramps said that's all we can do. You?"

My heart thumps.

"There's something else I need to tell you," I say, "but I'm scared. You might hate me again."

Ned touches my hand. He holds my finger like the Bean does.

"I couldn't hate you, Jemima Puddleduck," he smiles. "You just make me cross sometimes, that's all. Sometimes it's hard to understand you."

"Well," I say, chewing my nail, "you know Tory's accident? She fell because she was trying to stop *me* from jumping out. I thought if *I* fell out of the window and hurt myself badly enough, then my dad would *have* to come back home. I know it was a stupid thing to do, but the idea just came to me in a flash and swept me away. I thought I could fly like an angel. I didn't have time to think. There – I said it!"

Ned's eyes flash bright.

"You're crazier than I thought, Jemima Puddleduck," he says. "Truly, truly mad! Still trying to rearrange the alphabet. You need to get that if you're patient

243

the alphabet won't need rearranging. Things will work out. One way or another."

His eyes search for mine.

"I *am* next to U."

He looks at my arms. He traces his finger round an inky angel. He peers at me from under his fringe.

"Can we send some?" he says. "You know, for my gramps?"

I stand in front of the window. The wind is wild outside. I stare it straight in the eyes. "I'm not afraid of you, wind," I say.

Ned stands behind me. I lift my arms up high and together we set a million angels free. They rise from the inky blue shadows and shimmer as a radiant flash of brilliant white; their great wonderful wings swoop and soar through the sky to Gramps, who is sleeping on his star. To Dad in the dawn of the desert. To Kitty and James and baby Joan. To Derek and Granny. To Tory Halligan. To Jess. To Mrs Bostock. To Mum. To Milo and the Bean.

To everyone who ever died.

To everyone alive.

Chapter 24

It's a nutty one. My favourite...

The Bean's name is Joe. Mum decided in the night. But to us he'll always be the Bean.

"I like it," says Mum. "It'll look nice on a birthday card. *Love from James, Bex, Jemima, Milo and Joe.*"

If I had my way I'd call him Gabriel or Michael or Raphael because the Bean is an angel here on earth.

After school I call my mum.

"I'm going to the hospital," I say. "I need to talk to Tory. Then when I get home I'm going to tell you the truth."

The hospital rises up from the ground like a great grey monster with a thousand window eyes blinking in the sun. I stand in front of those eyes. "I'm not afraid of you, Tory Halligan. I'm not afraid of the truth."

Tory is out of intensive care. She's propped up on pillows in the children's ward. Paper birds hang from the ceiling and fly around her head. Painted rainbows stretch across the walls with pots of gold at the end.

Tory blinks when she sees me.

"Um, hi!" she says.

"Hi!" I say back.

I sit on the edge of her bed and then I'm not sure what to do next. I've never visited anyone in hospital before and it's weird being here with Tory. I look at her. She looks at me. My tummy flips. We're both waiting to see who will speak next. I feel really awkward and I'm scared my words are going to clog up in my throat. The silence between grows too long, so I offer her one of Mrs Bostock's chocolates. I still have plenty of them in my blazer pockets.

I take a deep breath.

"I needed to come," I say, "to say sorry. What I did was really stupid."

Tory puts the chocolate in her mouth. She fiddles with the golden wrapper. She stares at her hands.

"I feel embarrassed," she says. "I should be the one saying sorry. I don't know what happened to me. I just got carried away and turned into this completely spiteful she-devil. What I did to you was really mean."

"I thought you were dead," I say. "When you were on the ground all quiet and your leg was twisted. I was really scared."

"Why did you try to jump?" she asks. "What were you trying to do?"

I sigh.

"I've been trying to get the army to send my dad back home and I thought if something bad enough happened then they'd have to. I miss him so much when he's away, I can't bear it. And I get scared about stuff. So I began this Bring Dad Home mission. I started with the angels – I thought they might keep him safe – then it was the fire alarms. It was me who set them off and I was hoping Mrs Bostock would get really angry and expel me, but all she did was give me these."

I show her my pocket full of bright chocolates.

"Then I thought, *I know, I'll pretend I'm really ill*, so I tried to make myself have a fever and stuff. I thought about breaking my arm. I thought if I could get to be here, in hospital, like you, then he'd *have* to come home."

Tory's eyes are wide.

"You must REALLY want him home," she says, "to do all that."

"I do," I say, "a lot."

"But don't you think it's a bit extreme, Jemima? I mean, he will come back eventually." She smiles. "My dad would think I was completely crazy if I tried to hurt myself like that for him."

"My dad will think I'm crazy too," I say, "if he ever finds out."

"You're even freakier than I thought, Jemima," she says. "You're totally freakily bonkers!"

"I know," I say. "I can't help it. It's just how I am. But it gets worse. So then you and me were at the window and I was so, so angry with you. For a moment, I really hated your guts and if I'd have followed that hate I might have pushed you, Tory, because in that split second I did want you dead. It's true and I'm sorry for that. I'm really, really sorry. That's what's so scary. What happened was bad enough, especially for you, but I keep thinking about what *might* have happened. You

248

keep giving me bad dreams. I keep seeing you tumbling like a white ghost through the air. But anyway, we were at the window and I think I knew, deep down, that I *wouldn't* push you, but suddenly I had this crazy idea. I thought, *This is it! This will definitely Bring Dad Home.*"

We look in each other's eyes. She's waiting for the final bit of my story.

"I thought I could fly like an angel," I whisper. "I knew it would hurt when I hit the ground, but it felt worth it to see my dad."

Tory stares at her hands. She fiddles with the chocolate wrapper.

"He's lucky to be loved so much," she says. "But he'd never want you to do that. It's seriously extreme, Jemima. I mean, jumping out of the window!"

"I know," I say, "and I feel really bad about the fact that it was you who ended up getting hurt. I was really stupid. I *am* crazy."

I twiddle my chocolate wrapper round and round my finger and make a tiny purple goblet. I balance it on my palm and offer it to Tory. Granny's words are spinning in my brain. *Backbone, Jemima, backbone!* I swallow hard and look Tory in the eye.

"I just need to say that it really hurts my feelings when you say mean things about my dad being in the army. And when you laugh about my clothes. And my presentation and stuff. Your words confuse me. They make me feel lonely."

She drops her head.

"I know," she whispers, "and I'm sorry. I don't know what gets into me. I'm spiteful and horrid to everyone. I think I just get really bored or something and I take it out on everyone else. But it's true, a part of me *is* curious about you, Jemima, and a bit fascinated by... you know... your weirdness and everything."

I hand Tory another chocolate. It's wrapped in red. It's going to be crunchy.

"I don't feel weird inside," I say. "I just feel like me. I can't help it. It's just how I'm made. I guess we just have to get used to the fact that everyone's different and that that's OK. It doesn't make them wrong."

She nods. She offers me a grape. The ones Mum and I bought her.

"And the Ned thing," she whispers. "I'm sorry about that too, because it's obvious he likes you. I don't even fancy him, but I just got so jealous, I had to try to pull him away from you. I don't know why, but I always *have* to be the best, and the first. I hate it if I'm not number one. So I guess I'm pretty crazy too!" She sighs.

"And I had some pretty mad dreams while I was unconscious. It's weird knowing I slept for a whole week and missed everything."

Tory's mum and little sister appear with at least a hundred shiny pink balloons. I slide off the bed. I give her another chocolate, a yellow one. It's a toffee.

"I'd better go," I say, looking at the balloons. "See you around, Tory, and I hope you get better soon. I really do. All the girls at school are missing you loads. They don't know what to do without you."

And then I walk away.

On my way home I feel different inside. A little bit braver. A little bit taller. I bend down to tighten the laces on my boots. My dad would be shocked if he could see them now. I haven't cleaned them in weeks. They're all dull and dusty. I can't wait until he comes back home and we can sit on the back doorstep to polish and talk and I'll tell him I've discovered that weird isn't really weird at all. Weird is just different. I skip up our front path. I haven't skipped in ages. I like different, it's OK.

When I go indoors, Granny makes a cup of tea, then takes the boys out for a walk and leaves Mum and me to talk.

Mum gets out the special shortbread biscuits. We press our fingers in the sugar. We let the tiny crystals slowly melt in our mouths.

"I'm sorry," I say, when I've finished my story. "I got muddled up. I was angry with the army and with Dad and with you."

"Oh, sweetheart!" Mum says, wiping sugar from my chin. "I know you miss Dad, but I didn't know things were that bad. I should be the one saying sorry. I think I should get the award for being the worst parent in the world. You could have hurt yourself really badly. I can't believe I missed the signs. I miss Dad so much when he's away it's hard to be patient with everyone. It's hard to even notice what's going on. Inside my head I'm screaming at the world because I need him here. Then I take it out on you."

"Do you really think I'm unhinged?" I say.

Mum laughs. Her eyes look so tired and sad. "I'm

the one who's unhinged!" she says. "I'm so sorry you heard those things. I was just letting off steam. Mums worry about everything and everyone, Mima, and sometimes we say stuff in the heat of the moment that we don't mean. I didn't ever want to hurt you, sweetheart."

I dig in my blazer pocket and pull out a chocolate. It's wrapped in shiny purple. It's a nutty one. My favourite.

"For you," I say, giving it to Mum.

Then she pulls me on her lap. I feel huge compared to Milo and the Bean. My legs are everywhere. My elbows jab in her ribs.

"My beautiful baby girl," she says, holding me so close I can feel her heart beating under her skin. "My beautiful Mima. I do love you."

Chapter 25

For the first time in ages things feel normal...

I have to do my presentation in three days' time and all I have are a few dusty old boards and not a lot to say. I pull the boards from under my bed and dust them off.

Mmmm, what to do?

I pull on my gas mask. I lie on my bed. I think.

I pull out my laptop and give fate just one more chance.

I type *Derek – Canada – Blitz – Boat* into Google. I can't believe my eyes. There is his name. Right at the top of the page!

It's Derek *Bech*, Granny. Not Derek Bach!

My heart skips a beat. I read on. There's so much information about him.

On 13 September 1940, nine-year-old Derek Bech and his family set sail on a ship called the SS *City of Benares*. They were heading to Canada, to escape the war. Just like Granny said. Then, on the evening of 17 September, a German torpedo hit the ship. It sank. There were more than ninety children on board and seventy-seven of them drowned.

My excitement slides away. Like oil in a pan.

Poor Derek.

Poor Granny.

He most likely drowned. I flick an angel off my arm. "Fly to Derek," I whisper.

Then I type in Derek, Barbara and Sonia Bech, just to find out more and my eyes can't believe what they find. They're splashed all over Google. And in big bold words it says, *Derek Bech: survivor!* He survived! Derek Bech survived! Seventy-seven other children died, but Derek Bech and his sisters and their mum all survived! Apparently, Barbara managed to get on a lifeboat, but Derek and Sonia and their mum had to cling on to a raft, in the freezing water, all night long, before they were saved. The ship had been like a palace, with amazing food and mountains of ice cream, then late one night a big BOOOOOOOMMMMMMMM sound filled the ship and it started to sink. They never did get to Canada and Derek Bech has lived in Bognor Regis all this time! Granny could have found him if she'd tried a bit harder.

Google is full of fascinating and wonderful information.

Eventually, I stumble across an article from the BBC. It's called *The Children of the Doomed Voyage* and a man called Steve Humphries has made a film. I'm dizzy with it all. I'm scared he might be dead. He must be really old.

I do some quick maths. If Derek Bech was nine years old in 1940 that means he'll be eighty years old this year. Same as Granny. Of course, she already told me they were born on the same day.

I want to leap up and tell Granny. But I want to keep Derek like a sweet surprise. A thousand butterflies fly from my heart.

I send an email.

Dear Mr Humphries,

I'm trying to trace Derek Bech, a survivor from the SS *City of Benares* tragedy and wonder if you know if he's still alive? And if he is alive, how I might contact him?

He was my granny's childhood sweetheart and I'm hoping to reunite them.

Thank you,

Love from

Jemima x

I press send. I wait.

At suppertime I'm a jumping jellybean.

Granny says, "What's up, pet? Got ants in your pants?"

Then Milo pipes up. "No, Granny, she's got jelly in her belly!"

Then the Bean does a massive fart and we all fall about giggling.

For the first time in ages things feel normal. The house feels normal. Well, normal for us, that is! And my mum is even smiling. I'm smiling too.

A beautiful pink flower of hope opens in my heart.

Then my phone goes.

Pip. Pip. *My mum told me U tried 2 jump! That proves it. U really R mad!*

I text back.

Pip. Pip. *Maybe, Jess. But Truth is better than Dare.*

At bedtime I check my emails.

Nothing.

In the morning I check my emails.

Nothing.

Only two days left to go.

I have a serious talk with Granny.

"Granny," I say, "I need your help. I really need you to come to school on presentation day and talk about the Blitz. Otherwise my presentation will be rubbish."

Granny looks at me. She pours some tea. Her spoon clinks against her cup.

"Oh, pet," she says. "I don't know. It was all so long ago. I'm sure no one will be interested. I'd rather not."

"Please, Granny?" I plead. "I really *need* this."

At lunchtime I find Ned. His eyes are red-rimmed. He's in the library choosing readings for his gramps's funeral. He's getting used to foster care.

"Don't have any choice, do I?" he says. "But I'm

definitely going to boarding school. They just need to find me a guardian for the holidays."

I tell him about my plan.

"I'm not doing my presentation," he says. "Mrs Cassidy understands. It's all a bit much, really."

After school I check my email.

And there it is. Fate is working well.

Dear Jemima,

How lovely to hear from you and I'm delighted to be able to tell you that Derek Bech and his two sisters, Barbara and Sonia, are all alive and well. I made a film about the survivors of the disaster a few years ago, and if you're interested to learn more I could send you a copy.

Derek has been very happy for me to pass on his details over the years and I'm sure he'll be delighted to hear from you. He still lives in Bognor Regis. I've written his address and phone number below.

What a wonderful thing to do for your granny. I wish you good luck with their reunion.

Best wishes,

Steve

I'm a firework inside. Totally fizzing with joy. I write Derek's number on my hand, creep into Dad's study and shut the door.

I dial the number. My heart starts pounding in my chest. What am I *doing* phoning a total stranger? What am I even going to *say*? Derek might be cross. He might not be as lovely as Granny remembers. The phone starts ringing and I'm so nervous I want to throw it down. *You have to go through with this, Jemima*, I say to myself. *You can't back out now!*

He picks up his phone.

"Hello!" he says. "Derek Bech speaking, can I help you?"

I'm shaking like a leaf.

"I… I'm…" My voice won't work.

Come on, Jemima! Speak! It's Derek Bech in Bognor Regis! It's actually him!

"Hello?" says Derek. "Is anybody there? Look, if this is a prank call you can forget it and push off…"

And then I find my voice. I speak up loud and clear and Derek Bech and me stitch and weave a plan.

*   *   *

When presentation day comes it's the last and least worrying thing on my mind. I'm not scared. I'm not even that bothered.

Callum Richardson's presentation is still quite boring. He shows us his football kits and tells us all about the life of being a fan.

Mrs Cassidy stifles a yawn.

Hayley's presentation is amazing. She has little bowls of melted chocolate and cream. She wears an apron all covered in flowers. She has big wooden spoons and chocolatey lips and hands out coco-dusted truffles at the end.

Jess is full to the brim and over the top with dolphins when it's her turn. She's already adopted one called Splash and her mum is taking her to Florida in the summer to see it for real life. Her dolphin collection has grown to aquarium heights and she hands them out for everyone to see, for us to marvel at their glittering glory.

When it's my turn, I face the class with a crystal voice and speak. I focus, focus, focus. I stand up tall. I show the class my rain-grey boards full of sparkles and hearts. I tell them about missing my dad. I tell them about Granny and Derek and the incredible story of the SS

City of Benares. I tell them about how many children died and about how war breaks hearts. I show them my angels. I tell them about hiding in my dad's wardrobe. I tell them about setting off fire alarms and pretending to be ill and wanting to fly. I tell them everything and that Truth is better than Dare.

When I've finished there isn't a dry eye in the room. I have touched them with my truthful words. And Mrs Bostock is standing at the back, listening with a smile. She raises her arms up high when she claps. She unwraps a shiny chocolate and pops it in her mouth. It's a purple one. My favourite.

Jess shrinks down in her seat. She nods at me when I pass. We'll never be real friends, Jess and me, but hopefully now she'll leave me alone. Hopefully now we have a truce.

After school Ned is waiting for me at the gates. His eyes are shining.

"You were brilliant, Jemima Puddleduck," he says. "Truly brilliant!"

He looks at his watch. Time to go. Everything's working to plan.

"Thanks for your help, Ned," I say. "I couldn't have done it without you."

He smiles. "No problemo, Miss Puddleduck. No problemo!"

When we get home, we act like normal, as if nothing life-changingly earth-shattering were about to happen in our house. Granny is fluffing in the kitchen. Mum's doing spellings with Milo. Ned helps me make some tea. I pull the special shortbreads from the cupboard. I pop them on a plate.

Then the phone rings exactly according to plan. Everyone's ears stretch. They all think it might be Dad. Mum leaps up. I grab hold of her arm and pull her back in her seat.

"Let Granny get it," I say.

Granny looks up.

"Me?" she says.

Ned pulls his camcorder out of his bag. I want him to record this amazing momentous occasion for all of history to see and for Dad to watch when he comes back home and for Granny to have for ever. Ned pushes the red button. Granny gets up to answer the phone and puts the wonderful Beany boy in my lap. I press my finger on my lips to shush Milo and Mum.

"Hello?" Granny says. "Is that you, James?"

A pause that seems to last for ever fills our ears. My tummy flips with excitement. Granny looks puzzled for a moment and then her hand flies to her mouth. She takes a sharp breath in. She stumbles backwards and I quickly put the Beany boy in Mum's lap and leap up to find her a chair. Her eyes twinkle and shine like Christmas and a look of pure wonder spreads across her face. She smiles at me. She takes my hand and we thread our fingers together and hold on tight.

"Derek?" she says. "My Derek? Is that really you after all these years?"

Gentle tears of joy roll down her cheeks. Her face blooms pink and opens like a beautiful flower. She looks at me and mouths, "Jemima Taylor-Jones! I can't believe it! You're a real miracle-maker!"

And I almost can't believe it either. The real, actual Derek Bech is on the end of the phone and my granny is on the other. So much time has passed and here they are again, chatting like no time has passed at all! Seventy-one years later they are reunited by fate and well… maybe by a little bit of help from me.

Granny pulls the photo of the small boy with big solemn eyes out of her bra and kisses his tiny face.

"Well, pet," she says, laughing into the phone, "I've got a bone to pick with you, Derek Bech, see. You didn't keep all those promises you made me and neither of us are getting any younger, so what are you going to do about it?"

She laughs and they start to talk. They talk and talk all about the torpedoed boat and Barbara and Sonia and Bognor Regis and Wales and the war. They fill each other in on the past seventy-one years. They talk and talk and talk like they've never really been apart. And while they make plans for meeting up so they can talk some more and start keeping promises, the rest of us eat biscuits and dip our fingers in sugar and let the crystals slowly melt on our tongues.

All the wonders and the mysteries of life unfold. I still don't know if God exists or what makes wonderful things and terrible things happen in this world, but I do know I can't stop people dying when they need to die. I can't stop them doing what they love with their lives. I can't *make* my dad come home or change his job until he's ready. I can't make a baby be a girl when it's a boy or wake a girl from a coma until she's finished with her dreams. And I definitely can't stop a boy with halo hair and laces like vines from liking me, when the real truth is, he does, even if I'm weird or different or whatever.

But I do know I can stand up for love because love is the best and most wonderful thing in this life. I do know I can stretch my heart wider than the ocean and further than the stars and that I can stand up in front of a class and speak out with a clear crystal voice. That I can stand at the window to face the eye of the wind and say, "I'm not afraid of you."

I know I cannot control the secret mysteries of the universe because the universe and people's lives are not mine to rearrange.

I know that Truth is better than Dare.

I stand at my window and look out at the night. I hold my arms up high and set a million angels free. They flurry from my skin as inky blue shadows. They flap their brilliant white wings and soar as a magnificent blaze of love…

towards the stars…

around the moon…

heading…

straight…

to you. x

Acknowledgements

Thank you, Daniel – my wonderful IT support man, personal chef, foot masseur, hottie-maker, lover, husband and friend for your presence, your humour, your patience and your love. I love you so much.

Thank you to my parents-in-law, Len and Georgie Maryon, for sharing your childhood memories of war. And thank you so much for everything else you've shared with me and for being such amazing grandparents to Jane and Tim.

Thank you, my beautiful Jane, for styling Jemima! For reading and feed-backing and being my text advisor and for bringing so much love and so many angels to my life.

Thank you, my beautiful boys, Tim, Sam, Joe and Ben, for all your love and gorgeousness and support.

Thank you, Tim and Susie, for all the love and memories we share. To Paul for this wonderful thing we still have. To Dawne, for our true and wonderful friendship.

Thank you, Roseanna, for being such a patient and honest reader – telling me that something needed to happen was very helpful. Without that, this would have been a very boring book!

Thank you a trillion times, my lovely Agent, Eve, for your constant support and love. Thank you a trillion times, my lovely Editor, Rachel, for your commitment to getting it right, your gift for knowing what works, for your faith in me and your love.

Thank you, wonderful Rose, for managing all the millions of details and for your constant commitment, care and love.

Thank you, Michelle Brackenborough, for such a gorgeous cover design, I love it so much! Thank you everyone else from HarperCollins, for all your hard work and enthusiasm.

268

Thank you to the real Mr Derek Bech and his sisters Barbara and Sonia, for agreeing to have your real life experience of the SS *City of Benares* disaster woven into my story. It felt so important to honour this piece of history with the truth.

Thank you, Major Philip Nathan and Nikki, Isabelle and Oliver for the guided tour of Army life. I hope I got it right! And thank you, David, Rachel, Lauren and Aimee Somerville for doing the same. Thank you, Captain Oliver Stuart, for helping me answer difficult questions with care. Thank you, Lucy, for telling me all about e-blueys and telling me the kinds of things you write to your dad about when he's away.

Thank you, Steve Humphries, from Testimony Films, for putting me in touch with Derek and for sending me your film and the book, *The Children of the Doomed Voyage*. They were both so helpful.

Thank you, my lovely niece, Nurse Zoe, for helping me get the coma and stroke info right.

And thank you to all the people who I'll probably never get to meet – those who plant and cut the sustainable forests, make the paper, print the pages, wrap and pack and drive and stack and sell my books – without all of you *A Million Angels* would be left drifting in my imagination instead of being read by the world.

Thank you, Adam, for gently guiding me home to me.

I send a million angels to you all. xxx

MORE AMAZING
READS FROM
Kate Maryon

"It was just school to me. I'd been there since I was seven years old. But I'm not there any more, I'm here and I need to get on and get used to it, just like all the other changes in my life."

Liberty is sure there's more to life than getting good exam results and earning lots of money, but her super-rich, workaholic dad doesn't agree.
And when Dad's business goes bust and there's no money left,
Liberty's whole world is turned upside down...

"The page is staring at me waiting for words, but I don't even know where to start. I'd quite like to begin the letter with something like, Dear Mum, Thanks for ruining my life, but I don't think that's the kind of letter that Auntie Cass has in mind."

Tiff's sparkling world comes crashing down when her mum commits a crime. Packed off to live with family in the dullest place on the planet – and without Mum around – everything seems to lose its shine . . .

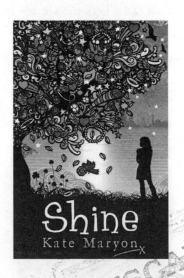

Shine

Kate Maryon x